ROBOTS VERSUS SLIME MONSTERS
An A. Lee Martinez Collection
A. Lee Martinez

Published by Fire-Breathing Rat Publications
Copyright 2013 A. Lee Martinez

Other Books By A. Lee Martinez

Gil's All Fright Diner
In the Company of Ogres
A Nameless Witch
The Automatic Detective
Too Many Curses
Monster
Divine Misfortune
Chasing the Moon
Emperor Mollusk versus the Sinister Brain
Helen and Troy's Epic Road Quest

Thanks to our Kickstarter backers

Alison Alvarez, Audio Mike Amman, Paul Angelosanto, Jan Arrah, Azhrei, Rodney Baker, Robert Bartsch, Sarah BaeHurst, Susan Bailey, Mark Baker, Jeffrey Barnes, Aaron Bartel, Jesse Baruffi, Sam Baskin, Jeffery Ericvonfluttenbyrd Beckman, Jan Beisenkamp, Shawn Belton, Katie Berger, Chad Bever, Jeremy Bort, Robert Bouthot, Megan Brackett, Aaron Bradford, Paul Bulmer, Michael Butson, Peggy Callaway, Melanie Carrin, Carter, Stephenaa Carter, Michael Carter, Michael Carter, Michael Cavaliero, Andrew Cherry, Chris, Nicola Claire, Rosemary Clement-Moore, Martin Conover, John Cooke, Kevin Corey, Kate Cornell, Richard Scott Crawford, Andrew D'Apice, Peter Darley, Kyle Anthony Davis, Russell Davis, Kevin Deenihan, Gary Denton, Gary Denton, Joe DeRouen, Michael Dial, Todd DiGiacinto, Dreamingsamurai, Lue Driver, Ralph A DuBreuil, Matthew Duda, Dustin, Steve Dwyer, Elizabeth, Eric, Joshua Evridge, Angela Adams Fleider, Duncan Fletcher, Tiffany Franzoni, Willian Fritts, Rick Fryar, Kaia Gavere, Kameron Gibson, Joshua Gillman, Giobblin, Donovan Glidden, Carlo Gliha, Karen Goetsch, Cathy Green, Cathy Greytfriend, Grumpyhawk, Carol Guess, Bill Gumina, Jonathon Haar, Craig Hackl, Julie Harden, Charles Harrington, Robert Harrold, Andrew Hayes, Michael Haynes, Sarah Heile, Juan Herrero, Bobby Hitt, Phil Holland, Nik Holman, Morgan Ineson, Dawn Jackson, Robert Jackson, Rolanda Jackson, Jason, Michael L. Jennings, Tabitha Jensen, Justin Jessel, Jester59388, Eugene Johnson, Justin Julian, Stefan Krzywicki,

Elise L., Kathleen Lafollett, Loa Ledbetter, Kevin Lee, Tristen Lee, Matt Leitzen, Angela Leone, Greg Levick, Neal Levin, Andrew Lin, Brian H. Littrell, Gary Lobstein, Zachary Logan, Kenny Louis, Kyle Lowry, Justin Macumber, Scott Macumber, The Mad Hatter, Stephen Manning, Joey Manley, David K. Mason, Herbert Mason, Joe Matise, Matthurlburt, Grace McCall, Don McCowan, Chanté McCoy, Richard McCreary, Charles McDougald Jimmy McMichael, Paul McMullen, Paul McNamee, Steven Mentzel, Rod Meek, Insa Miller, Rob Miller, James Minot, Monkeygritz, Felice Moreno, Wayne Morrison, Cathy Mullican, John Murphy, Eric Noble, Gloria Oliver, Rebeca Paiva, pdqtrader, William Pearson, David Peery, Pen Ultimate Productions, Tony Peterson, Noah Ramon, Webberly RattenKraft, Andreas Rauer, Adam Roberts, Antonio Rodriguez, Roque Rodriguez III, Elizabeth Rogers, Matt Russell, Jairo Sanchez, Margaret St. John, Shawn Scarber, Charles Scott, Gary Scott, Noel Petersen Seaver, Aaron Settle, Sonya M. Shannon, Michael Shelton, Amy Sisson, Nathan Skank, Crystal Skelton, Pamela Skjolsvik, David Sloan, Andreas Stahlbock, Noel Steinle, David Swanson, Jim Sweeney, Charles Tan, Tania, Robby Thasher, Tibs, Denis Trenque, Geoffrey S. Turi, Lisa Weinberg, Donald Whittington, Jeffrey Wikstrom, Lance Williams, Matthew Williams, Andrew Wilson, Robert Wilson, Jaimie Vandenbergh, VonEther, Philip VonNeida, Jeff Xilon, James Yu, the ZBBC, Zipthebunny, ZuZuBe

ADDITIONAL ACKNOWLEDGMENTS

In addition to the many fine Kickstarter backers of this project, I'd like to mention a few important people behind the scenes that made this collection easier.

First of all, there are the many fine writers of the DFW Writer's Workshop, who offered sage advice on how to make these stories better. (And they were pretty amazing to begin with, so that's saying something.)

Next, my lovely and talented wife, Sally Hamilton, designed the cover and did a hell of a job. To all you aspiring writers out there, marrying a graphic artist is definitely the way to go. Just FYI.

Editing a book is tough, and I had some great backup in my ever-helpful Mom and Aunt Peggy. A better pair of copyeditors would be hard to find. Especially ones that work for free.

Russell C. Connor offered experience and guidance into my first step into self-publishing. Check him out at Darkfilament.com.

Finally, I'd be remiss if I didn't thank you for buying this collection. Writers only get paid to write because people care enough to buy their stories to read. So thanks for caring enough about animated witch's brooms and talking gorillas to keep on buying stories about them. You keep buying them, and I'll keep writing them.

Table of Contents

Bigfoot Dreams 9
Wizard Bait 25
Penelope and the Willful Blade 47
Greyback in Blue 67
Death, Dust, and Other Inconveniences 89
Work Ethic 109
My Dinner with Ares 129
Pizza Madness 147
Cindy and Cragg 161
Imogen's Epic Day 179
Afterword 201

BIGFOOT DREAMS

Gil's All Fright Diner

I've developed a strange fascination with the Animal Planet *reality show (in the loosest definition of that word)* Finding Bigfoot. *If you haven't watched it, I can't recommend it because it's a show built entirely on the principle of wandering through the woods and NOT finding bigfoot. Somehow, they've managed to squeeze several seasons out of it. I find the show alternately amusing and frustrating, but it did inspire me to write a bigfoot story. So there's that at least.*

Bigfoot was going to kill Clinton.

He tripped wildly through the forest, running in no direction except away. In those flickering moments between panicking, he realized he should head back to the trail if he was going to find his way out of here, but he was hopelessly lost already. Even if he did regain his wits, it was too late for that.

If he'd been in the right state of mind, Clinton would've remembered that time he'd gone camping as a seven year old boy and how he'd seen a sasquatch. No one had believed him, and after a while, Clinton didn't believe it himself. Just the overactive imagination of a kid who didn't know better.

Now that thing he'd mostly forgotten about had caved in Billy's head with one blow and had been in the midst of tearing Jefferson to pieces when Clinton, in his mad fear, ran. Jefferson's screams and the howls of the bigfoot had long ago faded, and now, all he could hear were his own ragged breaths, whistling through his deviated septum.

If he got out of this, he swore he'd never go camping again. He'd stay in town, and he'd never even step into a goddamn public park if he could help it. Then he tripped over something, struck his head against a tree, and writhed in the dirt for a few moments.

Something big and black moved in the corner of his vision. The hairy giant bent down and sniffed him. Clinton shut his eyes tight and tried not to breathe in hopes of . . . well, he wasn't quite certain. But it was either that or run for it, and running would've been a waste of time.

"Is he dead?" asked someone from behind the bigfoot.

"No," said the bigfoot.

Clinton opened one eye and looked into the bright yellow eyes of a wolf's face. The wolf stood up and put its hands on its ample gut.

"Holy shit," said Clinton. "You're not bigfoot."

The skinny guy in overalls beside the wolf laughed. "No shit. You ain't never seen a werewolf before?"

He cocked his head to one side and sighed.

"Aw, hell, I was just giving him a hard time," he said to no one.

He bent down and offered his hand. "Let me help you up there. Looks like a nasty hit you took to the head."

The werewolf fell to the forest floor and started sniffing around.

"Please, don't hurt me," croaked Clinton.

"You can relax," said the skinny guy. "Duke doesn't hunt humans. Too easy, right?"

The werewolf chuckled.

"Hell, man, you don't even got a gun on you," said the guy.

"Fishing," said Clinton. "I was fishing. We were fishing." He grabbed the guy by the suspenders. "We have to get out of here. There's a monster out there." He glanced at the hulking werewolf. "Not like a friendly one either. It killed my friends. I think it's still after me."

Duke sniffed Clinton's neck and armpit. "The stink of fear you're putting out, I wouldn't be surprised." When Duke spoke, every word was a coarse, sharpened thing. It didn't ease Clinton's terror.

Both the werewolf and the guy turned their heads in the same direction and grumbled.

"Yeah, you're right," said the guy. "S'pose a little compassion is in order."

"Who are you talking to?" asked Clinton.

"My girlfriend. You can't see her cuz she's a ghost."

"Oh." Clinton backed away from the lunatic until he pressed up against a tree.

"You're running from a bigfoot, talking to a werewolf and a vampire," said the guy. "But ghosts . . . yeah, that's crazy."

"You're a vampire?"

The vampire cleared his throat and smiled, showing a pair of fangs. "But don't worry. I don't bite people unless they deserve it."

"Oh God," said Clinton. "Is everything in these woods a monster?"

"Monsters, he says." The vampire sighed. "We ain't been nuthin' but unfailingly polite to you."

He nodded at something his ghost girlfriend said.

"I know he didn't mean nuthin' by it, but it's still an insensitive word."

Clinton attempted to slink away, but Duke's giant, clawed hand clasped him on the shoulder. "You should stick with us if you want to live."

Staring into the toothy maw of the wolf's head, Clinton didn't feel particularly safe.

Robots Versus Slime Monsters

Somewhere in the darkened forest, a chilling bigfoot yowl pierced the night. It could've been a mile away. Or just behind the next bush.

"Oh God. It got Billy and Jefferson."

"Friends of yours?" asked the vampire.

"Sort of. I mean, not really. We don't hang out a lot. But Jefferson wanted to go fishing and talked Billy and me into it. We were just camping by the river, bullshitting. Then it just came out of the dark and—"

He closed his eyes and concentrated on the black nothingness rather than the horrible sights and sounds swimming around in his memory.

"They're dead. Aren't they?" he asked.

"'Fraid so," said the vampire. "And you'll be next if you get too far away from us."

"But why? I didn't think bigfoots were supposed to be dangerous."

"They aren't normally. Most of the time, they're docile nature spirits. They slip in and out of the spirit world, walking between planes the way we walk between rooms."

"Spirits? But I thought they were animals."

Duke and the vampire laughed. "What kind of goddamn sense does that make? Giant ape men strolling around in the forests, somehow not leaving a trace behind? No, they're more like ghosts, but ghosts that were never alive. Just sort of have always been here, crossing between worlds, peeking into ours when they get curious. Harmless, really. Except sometimes, one of the damned things decides it wants to be human, and the only way to do that is to eat the hearts of three humans under the light of the half moon."

The canopy was too thick to see much of the sky, but he remembered the light of the half moon shining down on the camp.

"Shit."

The vampire said, "Don't worry. You're safe as long as you're with us. Duke is more than a match for any bigfoot. And that's why we're here anyway. Duke's got a mad on to kill this rogue squatch. Don't know why."

Duke growled.

"Yeah, yeah. Your duty as an emissary of the forest and humanity. Or some other bullshit. Honestly, I just think it's because you can't resist a good scrap."

Duke chuckled, and the laugh sent a chill through Clinton's bones.

Another howl broke the silence, and it was joined by a second. Then a third. Then too many to count.

"Okay, now that sounds like it could be trouble," said the vampire.

He paused.

"Easy for you to say," he said to his ghost girlfriend. "You're immaterial."

Duke crouched on all fours. His ears fell flat. The black fur on his back rose. Unseen things rattled around in the foliage.

"Run," he said.

Clinton hesitated. "But you said—"

"I said run!" roared Duke.

A massive creature burst from the dark and came barreling at Clinton. Duke intercepted, plowing into the bigfoot with enough force to knock the creature into a tree, nearly uprooting it. The werewolf pinned the bigfoot against the tree and sank his snapping jaws into its shoulder. It bellowed, and its cries were echoed by a dozen other invisible monsters.

The vampire grabbed Clinton's arm and pulled him in the opposite direction. Or so Clinton hoped. He couldn't pinpoint a direction. The calls seemed to be coming from everywhere and nowhere at once. Monsters rustled in the dark.

"Not really your night is it, buddy?" said the vampire. He dragged Clinton through the woods. There were times Clinton would've tripped and fallen, but the vampire was stronger than he looked and kept Clinton going.

The bigfoots continued to close in, and all he could think was that they weren't going to make it. The monsters were going to catch him and drag him back into the woods. He couldn't let that happen. He didn't want to go back. Not ever again.

"I think the road's back this way," said the vampire.

A bright red sasquatch came out of nowhere and belted him across the jaw. He tumbled to lay in a heap. His head twisted at a weird angle, and by all rights, he should've been dead. But he groaned and struggled to stand.

The bigfoot beat its chest and grabbed for Clinton, who fell back just out of reach. Duke launched himself from nowhere, and the werewolf and his opponent tumbled into the dark.

The vampire mumbled through a broken jaw as his head rolled around limply on his shoulders. His posture was strange, slumped, off balance, with his right arm sticking out at an angle, like he was holding onto something.

Must've been his ghost girlfriend holding him up, decided Clinton.

Two more bigfoots emerged from the woods.

"Shhttt," said the vampire with his fractured jaw, just before one of the creatures grabbed him by the legs and smashed him into the ground several times, breaking more bones. The shattered vampire twitched in the bigfoot's grasp.

"Fk yi," he drooled.

The bigfoot dropped him. The second one seized Clinton and threw him over its shoulder. They were dashing through the darkened woods within moments, and out of the darkness, there were suddenly seven or eight more of the creatures. Even as the cold night air erupted from their nostrils in white puffs, they were as silent as ghosts.

A sharp pain ran through him as the world changed. The darkened woods filled with a soft blue light, and the forest opened up for the pack of sasquatches. The trees twisted into strange shapes. The overwhelming scent of honey and smoke filled the air.

Clinton didn't call out for help. It was too late for that. The bigfoots had taken him, dragging him back to their spirit world, the invisible realm behind what he'd always called reality. It was familiar yet strange at the same time, and he couldn't fight against them.

They reached a clearing, and the bigfoots deposited him with surprising gentleness on the ground. The night sky was a rainbow of colors without a single star in it. Just a half moon shining down upon him.

The bigfoots surrounded him. The leader, a large, gray-furred brute, growled at him. He could almost understand the creature.

His arm felt funny, and he rolled up his sleeve to see thick, white fur sprouting from his forearm. He felt his face. It was hairier, and it'd changed shape. His mouth was bigger, his teeth larger and flatter. He tried to speak, but could only grunt.

The sasquatches raised their heads and howled in a beautiful cacophony, and the gnarled trees swayed in rhythm with their rough chorus.

They were turning him into one of them.

Clinton scrambled to escape, but one of the creatures knocked him down. He tried twice more with the same results. He could feel himself slipping away. His mind faded as alien thoughts and instincts filled him.

A woman and a dog charged out of the brush. Neither of them were much to look at. The dog couldn't have weighed more than twenty pounds. The woman was armed with a baseball bat, but still stood several feet under the smallest of the squatches.

The terrier pounced onto the leg of the leader, and despite the absurdity of it, the bigfoot shrieked as if mauled by a lion. The other bigfoots ceased singing, and Clinton's mind returned. Not all of it. There was still something inhuman in there, but it was buried deep underneath.

The bigfoots intercepted the woman, but she knocked them all aside with one mighty swing. The laws of physics here were screwy because they didn't fall away. They hurtled into the sky and didn't fall back down.

She wound up for another swing. The dog joined her side. It lowered its head and growled, and the sound that came out was the rumble of a hellhound. The spirit world was a weird place.

"Who else wants some?"

The creatures readied to charge, but their leader raised his hand and grunted. Improbably, impossibly, one by one, they shuffled into the phantom forest, disappearing into worlds unknown.

"Are you all right?" she asked.

Clinton nodded. "I am now. Who are you?"

"I'm Earl's girlfriend. Cathy."

"The ghost?" he asked.

"Good thing for you too. Only a pair of ghosts could've followed you into this place."

"The dog's a ghost too?" he said. "Of course it is."

"I'd introduce you, but we should probably get back before the doorway closes. Hate to be stuck here."

The dog barked.

Clinton was worried they might not be able to find their way back, but the ghostly woods showed the way with a glowing trail. It was almost as if they place couldn't wait to be rid of them. He wasn't sure exactly when he crossed back into the real world. It wasn't an obvious moment. He only noticed that the monster under his skin faded and the fur disappeared.

He was human again.

"Thank you," he said to the ghost.

She was nowhere to be seen, but he thought she must surely still be around.

He wandered around the woods aimlessly for a few minutes until stumbling onto Duke and the vampire again. The vampire's wounds were mostly healed though he limped on shaky legs and his head was cocked a bit off center. The werewolf carried a corpse over his shoulder.

"Cathy found me," Clinton said. "If not for her . . . ."

He didn't finish the thought, not wanting to dwell upon it.

The vampire and the werewolf exchanged a glance.

"You want to tell him or should I do it?" asked the vampire.

Duke grunted.

"Tell me what?" Clinton asked. "They aren't coming back for me, are they? Oh Jesus, tell me you can protect me."

"They aren't coming back," replied the vampire. "They don't want you anymore."

He nodded to Duke, who dropped the corpse in front of Clinton.

It was him. The torso itself was a ragged mess, and one of the arms was missing. There was a hell of a lot of blood, and the face was a twisted mask of pain and terror.

But it was him, all right.

"'Fraid we got some bad news for you, friend," said the vampire.

"I don't understand."

But Clinton understood. Even before the vampire explained.

"Should've suspected as much by your scent," said Duke, "but thought it was just the stink of the other bigfoots on you."

"I'm not me," said Clinton coldly. "I'm the thing that killed me."

"Looks like it. Guess you got that transformation you were looking for. Maybe more of a transformation than you expected."

Clinton thought about his life. He remembered his wife, his two children. His dog. His house with the leaky water heater. His dead end job that he hated. It was all there, but it was all a lie. Memories stolen from a dead man.

"The other bigfoots weren't trying to change me into one of them," he said. "They were trying to change me back."

"Yep, guess the right thing to do would've been to let 'em," said Earl. "Little too late for that now."

The ghost said something. Clinton could almost hear it, but the rustling of the leaves was just loud enough to bury it.

"Hell, honey, I wasn't saying you did anything wrong. Just suggesting that running off into the spirit realm without thinking about it isn't something you want to make a habit of."

"I'm a monster." Clinton sat on the cool earth. He dug his fingers in the dirt. It felt all so real but hollow too. Like half a world. What mysteries had he traded away for this place? "You should kill me know."

Duke was there beside Clinton in an instant. The werewolf pressed his muzzle into Clinton's neck and sniffed his head for several long seconds.

"No squatch scent," said Duke. "No point in it now."

"But after what I did . . . ."

Duke snorted and turned away. "What you did made you human. I don't kill people. Not ones that don't deserve it anyway."

The vampire said, "The way Duke and I got it figured, you're not a bigfoot anymore. You're a man. That man." He pointed to the corpse. "And seeing as how that man has already had a pretty fucked up night, it'd seem especially fucked up to have to die twice in an hour."

Clinton laughed mirthlessly. "But I'm not him."

"Says who?" asked the vampire. "You got his body. You got his mind."

"But it's not real."

"Real as you let it be. Let me ask you, do you feel like you?"

Clinton nodded.

"Do you remember what it was like to be a bigfoot?"

"No, but—"

"Listen, I'm not gonna get into a whole metaphysical discussion on identity and the nature of the self. Philosophy isn't my strongest suit.

But near as I can figure, if you think like him and you act like him and you look like him—"

"Down to the scent," added Duke.

"Right down to the scent," continued the vampire, "then you're him. Or close enough to him that neither Duke or I would feel comfortable finishing you off. Especially since one of us went to enough trouble to risk her ectoplasmic ass chasing you into other dimensions."

He held up his hands.

"Hey, don't get mad at me for being worried about you. You're my goddamn girlfriend, after all."

"What am I supposed to do?" asked Clinton.

"Go home," said Duke. "Live your life."

"We could go 'round and 'round all night on this," said the vampire. "Way I see it, you've got two choices. You can keep sittin' here, feelin' sorry for yourself. Or you can live with what you've done, and try to make amends. Go home. Be a good husband and father. Do your job. You wanted this life. Shit, you killed this poor son of a bitch for it. Least you can do is take it now that you got it."

The werewolf grabbed the corpse and vanished in a blur. The vampire was less flashy. He stuck his hands in his pockets and sauntered away.

"We'll take care of your body for you," said the vampire. "You can probably get away with explaining the other two as a bear attack.

"Oh, and one more thing," he added. "Underneath it all, somewhere, you still have some bigfoot in you. It'll whisper to you now and then, and maybe one day, you'll get the urge to come back to the forest, to go home. That'll be up to you, I s'pose, if it's even possible, but at least have the decency to fake your own death or sumthin' before you do. Don't make this bastard look like some asshole who just abandoned his family." He smiled and nodded. "Best of luck to you."

He strolled out of view though Clinton could still hear the vampire arguing with his ghostly girlfriend.

"Damnit, Cath, I'm not going to apologize for calling you out on doing something stupid . . . ."

Clinton sat there in the forest, so familiar, so alien. He ran his fingers over his borrowed flesh, and thought about his failing marriage, his two ungrateful kids, his goddamn leaky water heater. He was a creature who had broken sacred laws as old as time to steal a life that the previous owner hadn't much cared for.

But he could make it work. He would make it work. He'd be a better person now. He'd be the person Clinton had never been. It might not make amends for his crime, but it was the best he could do.

The creature that was Clinton walked out of the forest, cautiously optimistic about his future.

He never set foot in the woods again.

WIZARD BAIT

In the Company of Ogres

The basic premise of In the Company of Ogres *was always about regular people just trying to make a living. That is a theme that pops up quite a lot in my books, and a lot of those regular people also tend to be monsters. It was* In the Company of Ogres *where I really had my chance to first explore the topic. This is just a tale of working stiffs who happen to be goblins, ogres, and orcs, and the trials and tribulations that come with the job. Also, it stars Ace, that most fearless goblin roc pilot, a character I've always been fond of.*

In a forsaken desert, atop a lonely mountain, a dragon's lair waited, and the mercenaries of Ogre Company rode a centurypede for one week to get there.

"I still don't know why we couldn't have flown," said Glunkins the orc.

Ace, their goblin driver, ignored him. He cracked the reins of the massive bug. Not because it noticed but because he liked the sound it made. The only way to steer the centurypede properly was to jam a pointy rod under its armored plates until it picked a random direction that coincided with where he wanted it to go.

He was sick of Glunkins complaining. No one liked riding a centurypede. They moved with undulating waves that made everyone a little queasy, and they smelled bad too. The heat wasn't helping. But soldiers went where the work was, and the centurypede was a one-beast caravan stretching nearly half-a-mile with unflagging endurance.

"Hey, it beats marching," said Martin, one head of a two-headed ogre.

"Indeed, it does, dear brother," agreed Lewis. "And a roc couldn't have carried us all."

"Could've carried me," mumbled Glunkins.

He hadn't stopped complaining since this trip had started, and Ace wished Glunkins would sit in the back. Way in the back, but Glunkins didn't like mingling with the other soldiers. Most of the bookkeepers in the Legion, contrary to expectation, were pretty fun guys. Glunkins was the exception.

Ace puffed on his pipe and stared straight ahead. Glunkins coughed pointedly. Ace ignored it, pointedly.

The mountain, a foreboding monolith of ebony stone, appeared on the horizon. Ace poked the centurypede. It grunted and slowed down. He poked it again, and it turned to the left a bit. A third poke got it to speed up and correct course.

The other hundred or so soldiers on the centurypede's back amused themselves with drink and games of chance. A week of burning sun had taken its toll on the soldiers' attitudes, but there were worse ways to get paid.

"Oh, we aren't going to have to climb that, are we?" asked Glunkins.

"We can always tie you to Lewis and Martin's back," suggested Sally.

She turned a bright, amused purple. The salamander was one of the few to enjoy this trip. She'd spent the majority of it sprawled across the centurypede's back, soaking in the heat and radiating it outward. Ace could feel her from here.

They reached the mountain a little after noon. Ace poked the centurypede to a stop, but it didn't really stop until it bumped into the tower of obsidian.

The great and terrible resident shrieked and launched itself from the cavern located at the peak. With great red wings and a howl that struck peasants dead, the creature landed with a crash beside the centurypede. The shockwaves rippled through the centurypede's body, and by the time they reached the farther end, several trolls and an ogre sitting too close to the edge were whipped into the air.

A. Lee Martinez

The red dragon glared at Ace with its gleaming black eyes. Ace looked back with the courageous indifference of a goblin who made his living staring into the maws of many, many things that could eat him.

"Is this all of you?" asked the dragon, her voice smooth and scratchy at the same time, like silk running across broken glass.

Ace stood in his saddle, which did not make him noticeably taller. "It's what you paid for."

The dragon balked, spitting a puff of fire as most dragons did when they balked. "I was told Brute's Legion was a professional organization. This is most unsatisfying."

"Yeah, things are tough all over," said Ace. "As it happens, there's an army of zillards amassing on the southern border of some country I've never heard of, but is willing to pay a hell of a lot of coin to have most Legion soldiers stationed there as a deterrent. Command has done some last minute reassignments. We're what they can spare, so you can take it or leave it. Or you can up your payment. Glunkins is the guy you want to renegotiate with."

Glunkins stepped forward and consulted a parchment full of tedious legal details. The dragon recoiled from the threat of paperwork.

"Very well. Though I thought you might not even make it. You really should make an effort to be more punctual."

"Take it up with customer service," said Ace. "We're here. Do you want us or not?"

"Yes, yes, you'll have to do. Have you been briefed?"

Ace nodded. "Standard treasure hoard guard detail while you're off at your big dragon orgy party thing."

The dragon frowned. "You make it sound so unseemly. The brood calling is a sacred ritual for the continuation of my glorious species."

"No judgment." The goblin grinned. "Do what you gotta do. But maybe if all you dragons didn't do this at the same time, we wouldn't be stretched so thin when the cycle rolls around."

"We do only as instinct commands. Believe me. We're no happier about it than you are. I assume you'll want to take a look around."

Ace called over Glunkins and Ulga, the chubby elf conjurer. They climbed onto the dragon's back, and she flew them up to her cavern while the other soldiers debated among themselves who would stay camped at the bottom of the mountain and who would have to scale to the top to guard the cavern entrance.

The dragon led Ace, Glunkins, and Ulga inside. She pointed to the glowing orbs fixed along the walls. "I've taken the liberty of installing a few lightstones. I don't need them myself, but I assumed you would." Mountains of coins and jewels sparkled beneath the twinkling golden stones. The hoard filled the cavern, and some of the valuables had even spilled out onto the ledge.

Ace whistled. "Is this all?"

"Oh, no. This is just the stuff I haven't gotten around to sorting through yet. The really valuable items I keep in the back."

"I don't suppose you have an itemized list?" asked Glunkins.

She tapped her temple with a long, black claw. "It's all in here."

It wasn't enough for the accountant, who walked among the treasures, scribbling estimates for his own records. Ulga picked up a handful of coins. She ran them between her fingers, bit them, dropped them in a special elixir and watched as the potion changed color.

"What's she doing?" asked the dragon.

"Just ensuring this is real treasure, not conjured fool's gold," replied Ace.

The dragon snorted. "It's all genuine, I can assure you."

"Assurances are great, but we need to protect ourselves. Had a wizard try to pull a conjuration scam. Hire us to guard a pile of phantom riches, disappear it in the middle of the night when nobody's looking then claim we need to pay for his losses."

"What can you expect from wizards?" she said. "Untrustworthy profession, I say. At the very least, it bestows upon them an unpleasant aftertaste."

"Eat a lot of wizards?" Ace asked, not because he was interested but just to make conversation.

"The occasional ambitious apprentice who comes seeking power. There's this rumor about dragon blood bestowing tremendous power to those who drink even a single drop of it. It's not true, of course, but still, they come, and they say eating a wizard now and then is good for maintaining the luster of one's scales."

Ulga tested a few more random samples of treasure while Glunkins took his cursory inventory. The accountant handed his estimate to the dragon, who signed the final bit of paperwork.

"Shouldn't be gone more than a week. Two, at the outside," she said.

"Take your time," said Ace. "We get paid by the day. Have fun at the orgy."

"It's not an orgy." The dragon spread her crimson wings and sighed. "Oh, never mind."

She soared off into the horizon.

***

Guarding a treasure hoard in the middle of a forsaken desert was every bit as interesting as Ace expected. The soldiers amused themselves by gambling or sleeping. The ogres in the assignment found some boulders to throw around in the traditional ogre game of throw the boulder. Ace didn't understand the rules, but there was a lot of hurling of giant rocks back and forth. Occasionally, someone would cheer, though he could never figure out why.

But on the third day, something finally happened.

"Do you see that?" asked Glunkins.

It was impossible not to see it. A great army marched toward the black mountain, kicking up clouds of dust. The force outnumbered the guard assignment by at least three to one. Ace poked the centurypede until it raised its head a hundred feet in the air, spilling soldiers off its back in the process. They groaned and grumbled from below.

"Sorry!" he shouted down as he used a spyglass to get a closer look at the approaching force.

"Skeletons," he said.

Glunkins groaned. "I hate necromancers."

"Don't we get paid extra for fighting necromancers?" asked Ace.

"I'm not sure."

Ace smiled. Glunkins knew pay standards to the last regulation. He only didn't know something when he wasn't happy with the answer, and he was only unhappy with the answer when it cut into the profit margins.

The army of the dead marched closer at a steady, slow pace, and the guards played cards, slept, and tossed boulders while they waited. Eventually, under the fading light of the setting sun, the undead horde reached the mountain.

Robots Versus Slime Monsters

The army was a motley collection of bones, clearly culled from a hundred different armies, judging by their assortment of equipment and tattered standards. The legion stood silently, ready for battle.

A giant's corpse with some moldering flesh still clinging to it stood at the forefront of the army. The titan fell to its hands and knees, shaking the ground. Several skeletons of descending size lined up beside the carriage mounted on the giant's back, and the necromancer used them as a staircase.

The gaunt, pale figure in flowing black and white robes held his twisted staff, and with the voice carrying the chill of the grave, he spoke.

"Surrender unto me that which is mine or join my legion."

"Uh huh," said Ace as he studied his hand of cards. "We'll be right with you."

"How dare you speak to me in such a manner? I am the Lich Lord Zarazath, and I have come—"

"You're undead, right?" asked Ace.

"I am beyond life and death, yes."

"Then one more minute isn't going to kill you. I've got a winning hand here."

Ace took two cards and ended up folding, after all. The goblin hopped off the centurypede and stood before the necromancer.

"What do you want?" he asked.

Zarazath leveled his staff at Ace. "You're in charge here?"

"Technically, he's in charge." Ace nodded to Glunkins standing to one side. "But he's a paper pusher, so it's me."

"Very well. I have come for the Pale Orb. Give it to me, and we shall have no difficulty."

"Hey, Glunkins is there a Pale Orb in the inventory here?"

Glunkins inspected the inventory. "Yep. One orb-comma-pale. Right here."

"Thusalah stole it from me," said the Lich Lord.

"Who?"

"The dragon," clarified Glunkins.

"Oh, well, you'll have to take that up with her," said Ace. "You should come back later."

"I think not. You are clearly outnumbered, and my army is beyond death. You have no hope of stopping me. Unless you wish to join my legion of the dead, you would be wise to step aside."

"What about you?" asked Ace. "Are you beyond death?"

Zarazath laughed. "Do you honestly think you can threaten Zarazath the Lich Lord? I am not just beyond death. I am death's master and . . . ."

His speech was cut short by the fall of a poorly thrown boulder. It crushed him beneath it. His legs stuck out and twitched for a while before going still. His army of skeletons collapsed into individual piles of bone.

"My fault," called an ogre. "A little help."

"We've got it." Martin and Lewis jogged over and rolled the boulder off Zarazath. The flattened sorcerer stared into the sky with his dead, yellow eyes.

"Mother always said necromancers were all talk," said Martin.

"Indeed, brother," seconded Lewis.

Zarazath cackled and sat up. He raised his staff, and his army of skeletons reassembled. Not all the bones were in the right places, but it didn't seem to bother them.

"Fools, do you think to strike the Lich Lord down—"

Martin and Lewis dropped the boulder on Zarazath once again. His army collapsed. They rolled it aside.

"Is he dead this time?" wondered Martin.

"Unlikely, brother dear," replied Lewis.

Zarazath raised his head. His empty eyes flashed red, and his staff sizzled with forbidden magic as his army pulled itself together. "Why waste your last fleeting moments in a futile—"

Ace nodded toward the ogre brothers. They used the boulder to hammer the Lich Lord into the dry, broken earth. Ace nodded again, and the boulder was removed.

"See here," said Zarazath, "this is no way to treat—"

They smashed the necromancer again. His limbs flailed wildly, and his army moved to attack. Ace yanked Zarazath's staff out of his hand. His legion of skeletons ceased moving and just stood at attention.

"Hey, give that back!" ordered Zarazath's muffled voice from under the boulder.

"Promise you'll go away if I do?" asked Ace.

"Yes, yes."

"Funny. Why don't I believe you?"

Ace nodded to Martin and Lewis, who proceeded to repeatedly bash the necromancer until they'd carved a crater into the cracked earth. When it became clear that Zarazath wasn't going to die, they decided to leave the boulder atop him. His one free arm flailed wildly as he mumbled curses.

Ace tossed the necromancer's staff to Glunkins to inventory. Zarazath's once intimidating undead force fell apart, one by one, into mounds of inert bones, aside from a one-armed skeleton in a loincloth carrying a broken sword who stood among the remains, looking forlorn.

Ace felt sorry for the skeleton and invited him over to play cards. The skeleton accepted, silently trudging to join the soldiers. He said nothing, and he didn't appear to understand the rules. This worked in his favor because, along with his unreadable leering skull, it was impossible to know if he was bluffing or not.

The skeleton scooped up the latest pot.

"I still say he's cheating," grumbled Glunkins.

"Ernie isn't a cheater," said Ace.

"You shouldn't name him. He's not a pet."

"Damn right he's not a pet," said Ace. "He's too good at cards to be a pet."

Ernie picked up the cards dealt to him, not bothering to look at them with his empty sockets. He stared straight at Glunkins, and the skeleton's jaws opened as if it to say something, but not a peep came out.

Glunkins grabbed what little money he had left. "Deal me out. But he's not keeping that."

"He won it fair and square," said Martin.

"That's not the point. What the hell would a skeleton need money for anyway?"

"He could buy a new sword," suggested Lewis.

Ernie's skull wobbled in a way not unlike a nod, though it might've been the gust of icy wind that swept across the camp.

A few snowflakes drifted down to melt away in the dirt.

Ace climbed the hill of bones that had been the titan skeleton and surveyed the clouds of white mist rolling across the desert. The temperature plunged, and the soldiers, who had spent days shying away from Sally's heat, all huddled closer to her.

Glunkins shivered. "Wizards. Always have to make a big production of everything, don't they?"

"If you could command the elements, wouldn't you?" asked Ulga.

The freezing fog rolled around, and it was impossible to see more than a few feet in any direction. A figure in white stepped from the mist. The squat dwarf had black hair, white eyes, and wore a gown of frost and ice that crackled as she moved.

"I am the Ice Witch Besberdin, and I have come for the Sword of Winters. Surrender it unto me, and I shall allow you to live."

"One Sword of Winters, check," confirmed Glunkins of the inventory.

"Thusalah isn't home right now, so it'd be better if you came back later," said Ace.

She raised her fist, and icy shards pelted the soldiers. "I command the powers of frozen hell. If I will it, you will be forever encased in ice, and your arms and courage could do nothing to stop it."

Ace blew into his hands, rubbed them together. "Have it your way. Sally, can you take care of this?"

The salamander stepped through the crowd of soldiers that had surrounded her. "I've got it."

"Fools!" The Ice Witch hurled icicle shards at Sally, who exhaled a gout of flame to melt them.

"I've been soaking up a lot of heat these last few days, lady," said Sally. "You'll have to do better than that. Anyone have an empty canteen I can borrow?"

Ulga waved her hands and conjured a plain, brown canteen that she tossed to Sally. Fire popped along the salamander's white hot body as she coiled around the witch. The wind howled as hail pelted the ground, and Ace's lost all feeling in his limbs. The unseen battle went on for some time and just when Ace was certain he was going to have a finger or two snap off, the storm vanished. The mist melted away as the desert heat came rushing back, nearly knocking everyone over.

Sally handed the canteen back to Ace. "One Ice Witch."

He shook the canteen. It felt only half-full. "This is all of her?"

"Most of her evaporated," said Sally. "That's just her frozen heart."

Ice was already forming on the canteen. Ace gave it back to Sally. "You should hold onto this."

Sally blew on the canteen with her hot breath, thawing the ice. "You got it."

"Now then," said Ace. "Who is up for another game? C'mon, Ernie. You have to give me a chance to win some of my money back."

The skeleton proved even better at rolling dice and had accumulated a small fortune by the next day. There was some argument, mostly from Glunkins, that Ernie wasn't alive and shouldn't be trusted, but everyone else thought he was a decent sort for a dead fellow. He was agreeable with nary a negative word to be said, which made him more popular than Glunkins.

By noon the next day, another army appeared on the horizon. This one belonged to a shaman who commanded a few hundred pygmy badgermen. The shaman sat on a throne borne on the backs of the hairy, snarling creatures.

"I've heard fighting badgermen is unpleasant," observed Martin. "They're very bitey."

The shaman, covered in layers of leather, with a necklace of skulls and a mad gleam in his eye, cackled.

"Give unto me the Bones of Swur or face death."

"Bones," said Glunkins. "Check."

Ace sized up the shaman and his army. The soldiers of ogre company were outnumbered five to one by the badgermen, though ogres were a match for a few dozen of the salivating beasts, so it wasn't as if numbers were all that mattered.

"Can't do it."

The shaman loosened his leather collar and wiped the sweat from his brow. The desert wasn't a good place for the outfit, but magicians of all sorts usually lacked common sense. He threw a bag into the air. It burst into a shower of red dust that settled on the badgermen at the forefront, who quintupled in size until they were even bigger than an ogre.

"Perhaps you might reconsider," said the shaman.

Ace nodded to his soldiers. They grabbed their arms and stood in a line before the frothing, shaggy giants.

Glunkins pushed his way through the crowd. "Let me handle this."

He approached the biggest of the badgermen. No one could hear what he said, but after a moment of discussion, the badgerman nodded, howled, and as one, the shaman's army turned on him. The shaman yelped as he was dragged under the horde of growling, yipping beasts.

"What'd you say to them?" asked Ace.

"I only pointed out that the Legion has more opportunities for advancement, a better pay grade, and a more reliable pension than working for a shaman."

A scrap of leather drifted by on the wind.

"Are you authorized to hire that many soldiers at once?"

"No, but they don't know that."

"Seems a bit dishonest," said Lewis.

"You're just upset because you were hoping for a fight."

"He has you there, brother," said Martin.

The badgermen made quick work of the shaman, who was bound

and gagged and presented to Glunkins as the first part of their employment application. He happily accepted before sending them on their way to the nearest Legion recruiting office with a letter of recommendation.

Not more than an hour after they'd settled that matter, storm clouds roiled above as hot rain fell from the sky. Thunder cracked, and a bolt of lightning struck, materializing a bearded figure. His robes shimmered, and his beard sizzled as static electricity sparked along it, causing the hairs to puff outward.

"I am the Storm Mage, and I have come for the Rod of Zorb. Give it unto me and I may allow you to live."

"One Rod of Zorb," said Glunkins. "Check."

Ace sighed. This was going to be a long assignment.

***

The dragon Thusalah landed with a crash at the base of her mountain.

"How was the orgy?" asked Ace.

She flapped her great wings in a shrug. "The selection of males was disappointing. I'm considering devouring my clutch after I lay it. For the good of the species."

The dragon surveyed the surrounding dessert. The necromancer wiggled helplessly under his boulder. The Ice Witch's canteen sat in a block of ice, managing a very localized snow flurry. The storm mage's rod blasted lightning bolts into the sky every thirty-four seconds. A thirty foot tall iron golem lay on its back, having crushed the alchemist who commanded it. The shaman lay bound and gagged. An immortal war warden lay pinned to the earth by a few dozen spears, swords, and axes. A naked sorcerer sat on a rock, cackling wildly to himself while conjuring flying lizards.

"Any trouble?" asked the dragon.

"Nothing we couldn't handle."

Glunkins had her sign and initial several forms.

"If you don't mind me saying so, ma'am," said Lewis, "is it really wise to have all these magical knick knacks laying about?"

"It does seem to attract a lot of magical power seekers," said Martin.

She smiled at the two-headed ogre. "That's entirely the point, young men. I collect them."

"I thought you didn't like wizards," said Ace.

"I'm not terribly fond of them, but they serve a purpose. Like roaches and strangleweed. Pesky things, true, but there for a reason. But an effort must be made to keep the wizard population under control. We dragons are great believers in preserving balance and too much of anything is bad for everyone. I'll keep these ones tucked away, reintroducing them when their numbers dwindle.

"I've found that all you really need do is collect a few enchanted baubles, sit back and wait for them to come to you. It's so much easier to maintain the bait than when I was in charge of hero conservation. The care and feeding of damsels is not as simple as you might think."

"I suppose you know your business," said Glunkins.

"Now then, you've done such a wonderful job. I must give you something for your trouble."

"We aren't allowed to take gratuities, ma'am. It's against Legion policy."

"Oh, but I insist." She smiled, showing rows upon rows of teeth, and everyone agreed it was unwise to offend a generous dragon.

She gave each soldier a handful of gold and jewels. Glunkins attempted to record the exact amount given each soldier but decided to let it slide after being buried up to his neck for half-an-hour.

After it was all done, Ace pointed out she'd forgotten Ernie.

"What good is money to a skeleton?" said the dragon.

"Exactly what I asked," said Glunkins as he shook the dirt out of his trousers.

"But I do have something here he might like."

She handed him a blood red sword. He waved the weapon wildly. It screamed with every stroke of the air.

"Now be careful with that," she said. "It's cursed that whoever uses it shall be burdened with greatness but suffer a terrible death. Not that the latter should matter much to you, I suppose."

Ernie climbed atop the centurypede, taking a seat beside Ace. Glunkins, put off by the way the skeleton kept staring at him, moved to the back. Way to the back.

Ace smiled, cracked the reins. "I knew there was a reason I liked you, Ernie."

Ernie's jaw waggled in a silent chuckle. Or perhaps it was only the wind.

PENELOPE AND THE WILLFUL BLADE

A Nameless Witch

I try not to play favorites with my characters. I really do, but since first creating Penelope the animated witch's broom, I've always loved her. A broom with no magical powers aside from the ability to move, a great attitude, and the most perfect sidekick a witch could ask for. (Sorry, Newt.) When brainstorming for this collection, I never had any doubt Penelope would get her moment to shine.

It was fair to say that the Willful Blade and I did not like each other upon first meeting.

My name is Penelope. I am a broom. I serve the Witch with the Unspoken Name, and I do so with pride. An enchanted broom is only as good as her bearer, and my witch was surely the best of her forbidden trade. I hadn't met all the witches in this world, but I assume it so until proven otherwise.

The bearer of the Willful Blade was a giant of a man, clad in gleaming armor, and we met him on a road leading to an evil warlord's fortress.

"Step aside, crone!" bellowed the warrior, even though my witch wasn't in his way. She was also secretly beautiful, which wasn't difficult to see aside from the fact that so few people bothered to look beyond the pointy hat and the dirt she rubbed on her face.

My witch said nothing and kept walking. She tended to ignore such blustering fools.

"You there, hag!" he shouted after her. "Didn't you hear me?"

My witch limped along, using me as a walking stick she didn't truly need. It added to the illusion, and I was only too happy to help.

"It's a wide road," she said. "There's room enough for two."

The warrior clanked after her. "You'd be wise to heed my words, crone. Farther down this road, there is a mad warlord who wields the power of the crimson mists. It is said it is a power no army can stand against and, if left unchecked, will threatens all the nearby lands. Perhaps the entire world. You'll find no mercy in his heart for even a wretch such as you."

Newt, my witch's familiar, snorted. A duck wasn't the most threatening beast, but he made up for it with a healthy dose of demon inside him. "Should I kill him?"

"Oh, he's harmless," said my witch.

The warrior ran ahead of us, and I hoped he would continue. Instead, he stopped and with a defiant laugh, drew his sword. "Harmless, am I? I carry the Willful Blade, a legendary weapon used by only the greatest of heroes."

He slashed the air with wide, clumsy strokes, laughing boisterously. I might not have thought much of him but I did note that his sword was magical. I greeted the sword in the silent language of enchanted objects.

"Hello."

The Willful Blade didn't reply. I took no offense. He was working at the moment, and like me, I assumed he took his duties very seriously.

Newt chuckled. "If you're not careful, you'll poke your eye out."

The warrior laughed again. Though he seemed a bit silly, he was at least a jolly fellow. That was more than I could say for his weapon.

His bearer followed along, continuing to slice at imaginary foes without much skill or grace. "But you need not fear, hag. Though I have heard tales that this warlord can devour nations whole with his deadly mists, I shall slay him with my mighty sword. For it is the only way to earn my honor and name."

He paused, giving my witch the opportunity to say something. Not that he was interested in what she had to say, but he was civilized enough to pretend like this was a conversation. But my witch said nothing. She was the kind of person to appreciate and cultivate a good silence rather than bury it under needless words.

The warrior was less comfortable with the quiet, and he attacked it with fresh vigor.

"You must certainly be asking yourself, why would I dare such a foolhardy quest? It is because generations ago, a wise wizard bestowed upon my family a great and powerful weapon. Ever since, each male, and some of the more adventurous females, have chosen to carry the sword upon coming of age and use it to vanquish an evil, thus proving themselves worthy of our noble ancestors."

The Willful Blade groaned, though, of course, only I heard him.

The warrior continued. "But until I have destroyed this evil, you would do well to turn back. This is no place for an old, withered woman. Though it soon will be."

He laughed once again. I heard some fear in the laughter, though I wasn't sure if he was aware of it himself.

My witch and her familiar simply continued walking.

"Didn't you hear me?" asked the warrior. "Why do you continue onward so heedlessly?"

"If you must know," said my witch, "I planned on killing this warlord myself."

"You? You must be joking, frail little thing that you are."

My witch smiled. She always enjoyed when people fell for her disguise. "I have my ways. And this warlord threatens my home and my friends. So I thought I'd take care of the problem before it became more of one."

She didn't say that she'd had a vision of this warlord's future, and how he was destined to fail in his quest for power. But not before ravaging the fort we called home. My witch had a fondness for the soldiers there, and she saw no reason to spend their lives so carelessly when she could solve it more efficiently. I didn't know her plan, but my witch wasn't one for plans. She mostly improvised, which was how witch magic worked best.

"I can see you're quite mad, hag," said the warrior.

"Oh, please, let me kill him," said Newt.

Most people were surprised by a talking duck, but the warrior was unimpressed. I suspected he wasn't impressed by anything but himself, and even then, this admiration smacked of shallow arrogance. The kind of bravado that might evaporate in a moment.

"Ah, I see now. You're some sort of witch, aren't you?" asked the warrior.

His sword groaned. "Figure that out all on your own, you half-wit?"

"He does seem a bit dense," I said.

"Nobody asked you," replied the Willful Blade.

"I'm sure it's no reflection on you," I added, trying to be helpful.

"Very kind of you to say, but I don't need the reassurances of an old broom. Especially an accidental."

There was a hierarchy among enchanted objects. The Willful Blade had been created by intentional magic. My enchanted nature was only a happy accident. Most intentionals couldn't help but be stuck up about it.

"You don't need to be rude," I said.

"You'd be in a poor mood too if you had to shepherd this idiot through his adventures. Although so far, those adventures have mostly been buying drinks in taverns. We did fight some bandits, though they were a scrawny, underfed lot."

I was fortunate that I liked my witch, and she appreciated me in return. Not all enchanted objects were so lucky.

A harsh wind picked up and blew across the road. It smacked of strange sorceries. My witch must have sensed it, but the warrior kept on babbling.

"I'm sure you're very good at getting rid of curses and inflicting or removing warts as the situation demands, crone, but this is dangerous business."

My witch stopped. She licked her fingers and tested the air, no doubt sensing the approaching malevolent magic.

"Ah, a very wise choice," said the warrior as he matched onward. "If you wait here, I'll return shortly to regale you with my tale of triumph."

Oblivious, he marched right into a creeping red fog that appeared from nowhere. It swallowed him, and there was a terrible clatter. The fog rolled forward and my witch used me to trace a line across the road. The mist nipped and prodded at her barrier. With each strike, it grew thicker and angrier, and within moments, it was all around us.

"Do something," said Newt. He was always nervous about those problems he couldn't slay.

She lowered her head and mumbled to herself. The fog recoiled. Only for a moment. Then it closed in, sharper and hungrier than before. It even growled.

"Interesting," said my witch.

The fog broke through her magical wards. My witch made not a sound, but Newt did yelp. The attack was over within seconds, and when the fog rolled away, disappearing as if it never was, my witch and her familiar were gone. Only her clothes remained. Not too far away, the warrior's empty suit of armor lay in a heap.

I flew high into the air to survey the landscape. The forest obscured much of the land below, but I had a sense of my witch if she was near. I sensed nothing. Quickly, I returned to the ground and poked through her clothes for any clue of what might have happened to her.

"You're wasting your time," said the Willful Blade, sitting beside the warrior's armor. "She's dead."

I ignored him as I swept some dust off the road. It helped me think.

"This is a fine way to end things," said the Blade. "I didn't like the idiot, but he deserved a more heroic end than that. I guess I should be going home then." He jumped in the air and floated away. "Here's hoping the next generation produces a more worthy hero."

I started down the road.

"Where are you going?" he asked.

"The warlord's citadel," I replied. "Where else?"

The sword stopped, tilted his blade at a curious angle. "Are you mad? Your witch is dead."

"I don't know that. Even if I did, it is my duty to continue her quest."

He zipped in front of me and held the flat of his blade in front of me. "Here now. You can't get attached to these bearers. They come and go. You have to take the larger view. You're a fine witch's broom. I'm sure you can find another to take you on."

"I don't want another." I hopped over him and continued on my way.

The Willful Blade chuckled. "Oh, she must be your first. The first one is always the hardest. But you'll get over it." He followed beside me. "I remember my first. Seemed like a terrible tragedy, but then along came the next bearer. Life carries on."

"You've lost others?" I asked.

"One or two. Or five. Not such a bad record, all things considered."

"You sound very cavalier about it."

"Not everyone is worthy of me," he said. "I can only do so much. Honestly, this one was the biggest fool by far, and while I regret his passing, I can't say I find it particularly surprising."

"My witch is not your warrior. She is capable and brave, and if there is a way to survive, she would have found it."

"Yes, I'm sure she's a very special witch," he said condescendingly. "I'm sure the next witch you find will be just as special in her own unique way."

Following my witch's example, I elected not to continue this pointless conversation. I increased my pace, soaring over the trees. The Willful Blade followed.

"Oh, don't be like that," he called as he trailed after me. "I'm just trying to spare you some pain. If you get unduly attached to a bearer, you're only going to get yourself hurt. Or worse, you'll blunder into a situation you clearly aren't prepared for."

I stopped, and he soared past me.

"What makes you think I'm unprepared?" I asked.

He dipped his point downward and swirled it in small circles. "I meant no offense, but you are just a broom."

I didn't reply, offering him a silence to either use for apology or to simply shut up.

"What are you going to do? Sweep this warlord and his evil magic into submission?"

I soared away, zipping through the trees. He didn't follow. Or so I thought. But when I reached the warlord's fortress, the Willful Blade floated beside me as I surveyed the place.

"Not many guards," he said. "Shouldn't be difficult to slip past them."

It wasn't. The fortress walls posed little problem for two of us since we could fly. In addition, both of us moved with absolute silence, and the patrols were on the lookout for soldiers and mercenaries, not a sword and a broom. We entered the fortress with even less trouble than I expected, and I hadn't honestly expected much.

It was only while moving down the halls of the keep that we finally ran into some difficulty. A pair of guards turned a corner, and we were almost taken by surprise. Fortunately, we had enough time to lean against the wall like a pair of ordinary un-enchanted objects. My hopes that the guards would keep walking proved optimistic.

"What's this?" asked the taller one. "Who left this here?"

"This isn't one of our weapons." The shorter guard reached out and picked up the Willful Blade. "But it is a fine sword."

"Here now," said the taller. "Give that to me."

The shorter waved the sword in the air. "I saw it first."

"You can't just call a fine sword like that."

"Says who?"

The men started arguing over who got to keep the Willful Blade in a way that was sure to bring more of guards.

"You wouldn't even know how to use it!" growled the taller.

"It's a sword. What's so tricky about it?"

And then, to prove his point, he stabbed the taller soldier in the heart. Except he didn't do the stabbing, as was made evident by the shocked expression on his face. He released the enchanted sword that hovered before him. It would've been simple for the Blade to finish him off, but it gave him a sporting chance to draw his own weapon. Instead, the soldier turned and ran, crying out for help. He didn't make it three steps before the Blade plunged itself in his back. The strike was masterful, and the poor soldier was killed instantly. It took the Blade a few moments to twist free of the impaled man.

"Impressive, isn't it?" he said.

"Except now there are two bodies we have no way of hiding."

The Willful Blade sighed. "What else could I do?"

As the saying went, when all you had was a hammer, it was easy to see every problem as a nail. I assumed the same logic applied to stabbing things when you were a sword.

We continued on our way, confident that, even when the bodies were discovered and the alarm raised, we'd have an easier time avoiding suspicion than most intruders. We ascended the keep with caution and managed to reach the top without causing any more deaths.

This seemed to disappoint the Willful Blade. I wasn't annoyed by his disregard for life, though I'd never been in favor of casual stabbing. It tended to make a mess, and I did so despise messes. We were all prisoners of our natures.

We entered the highest chamber of the keep. It was a cavernous single room without windows. Torches flickered on the walls, casting shadows in the murky gray. At the far end of the chamber, the warlord, clad in impractical armor, sat on a marble throne. The meticulously crafted suit gave him the appearance of a demon. The helmet itself was shaped in the sinister appearance of a skull with four curved, jutting horns. There was no sign of the face beneath it save for a red glint where the eyes would be.

"Here's my plan," said the Willful Blade. "You distract him. I'll wait to find a weak point in his armor and stab him. Then we can go home, having avenged our bearers."

Before I could argue, he slipped into the darkness.

I approached the warlord. He laughed. The chamber air grew chill. The dust, so much of it, swirled across the filthy floors.

"So you've come," said the warlord. "I am surprised. I wouldn't have expected it." He chuckled again. His helmet nearly fell off, but he held it down with one gauntlet. "You might as well tell your friend, that sword, that he's wasting his time. I have no weakness."

I took note of the amulet around his neck. It wasn't much to look at, which made it out of place on his otherwise fearsome appearance. Its gem was red, and if you looked closely enough, you could see mists swirling within it.

The Willful Blade remained in the shadows.

The warlord shrugged. "As you wish. But before you waste your time trying to slay me, I would say that I have a place for you in my organization. Both of you. An army is all well and good, and, yes, my magic is impressive . . ." He caressed his amulet. ". . . but a sword that can kill on its own would always be handy. And a broom . . . I can't think of a better spy."

"Is this the master you must serve?" I asked the amulet. "Or is he who you choose to serve?"

"You don't get it, do you?" replied the warlord. "The amulet doesn't serve me. I serve her."

"You understand me?"

He nodded, and his helmet clanked. "Just one of the gifts she gives me. For hundreds of years, she was passed from warrior to peasant, kings and knights and lowliest serfs and everyone in-between. She had within her great power and all she wanted to do was share it. And what did she get in return? They wasted her gifts. Always, they fell victim to their petty thoughts, their weak, short-sighted natures. So it was that greatness was always denied her.

"It could be the same for you now. If you think about it, what purpose did your bearers ever serve? Aren't you better off without them? Weren't they holding you back from your true destiny?"

The Willful Blade floated out of the darkness. "He makes a compelling argument."

I was disappointed he was so easily swayed, but convincing a sword to seek glory wasn't all that difficult.

"What's your answer?" asked the warlord. "Do you truly want to go back to being the tool of someone else? Or wouldn't you rather walk your own path?"

He held out his gauntlet as if to welcome me, but I stayed where I was.

"My path is beside my witch."

He sighed. "As you wish. Blade, send her off to join her mistress. Then we'll talk about making you general of my army."

The Willful Blade hovered closer. Enchanted objects weren't easily destroyed, but I sensed the power in the sword to unmake me.

"It doesn't have to be this way," said the Blade.

"No, it doesn't," I agreed.

He raised back. The edge of his steel, still stained with the blood of two men, flashed in the torchlight. In the moment before he struck, I hoped he might see the error of his way, but he was what he was. He could do no different.

He swung out in a blur, but I was faster. Only just. I ducked beneath the Blade's strike and danced out of reach of his attacks. We swept around the chamber in a deadly game. Once, I was too slow, and he sliced away a few bristles. It stung in a way I rarely felt. The pain surprised me so that I was nearly cut in half by his follow up. Still, I avoided the blow.

"Hold still," said the Willful Blade. "You're only delaying things unnecessarily."

The warlord, sitting atop his throne again, watched our struggle. His red amulet flashed in the dark.

I ducked to one side and hurled myself at him. I clanged ineffectively off his fearsome armor. The Willful Blade ceased his attack, afraid he might kill the warlord with a careless strike.

"You have spirit, broom," he said. "I'll give you that."

If there was one lesson I'd learned from my witch, it was that the mightiest foe could be undone by their own arrogance. He made not the slightest attempt to fend me off. I was only a broom. Amid all the ringing and racket of my blows, he only laughed.

Until I slipped under the amulet and with one deft flick, tore it from his neck.

"No!"

The amulet clattered not too far away.

The Willful Blade launched himself at me, but it was already too late. I slipped aside and he plunged with such force that he penetrated the warlord's breastplate, driving himself halfway. The warlord fell from his throne without as much as a dying gasp. His helmet rolled away to reveal a fleshless skull. It was no wonder he'd had such a hard time keeping it on.

While the Blade struggled to free himself from the armor, I floated over to the amulet. As she remained laying on the floor, I could only assume she lacked the power of independent movement.

"You don't have to pretend anymore," I said. "I knew it was you all along. The warlord never existed."

"He existed," she replied. "Once. But when he died, I realized I didn't need him. I saw no point in waiting for another to come along when I could just as well take charge of my own fate."

I could sympathize. Existence was a complicated affair for an enchanted object. It must not have been easy waiting for the right soul to come along.

"They're not all the same," I said.

"I can't go back to serving buffoons."

"That's your choice, I suppose."

The Willful Blade extracted himself from the armor and swirled in a few practice slashes.

"Finish her off!" said the amulet.

The Blade hesitated.

"Think of the glories awaiting you!" she said. "Think of the way creatures will tremble at the mere mention of your name, of the glorious carnage you shall unleash on a thousand battlefields!"

"Yes, think of it," I said. "Think of the blood spilt simply because you stopped trying to be anything other than what you are. Imagine a world where you are covered in gore, where your lust for death and glory is sated, where you sit beside the throne of this warlord on a heap of corpses. It is everything you've ever wanted, isn't it?"

The Blade lowered his point.

"What's wrong with you? Didn't you hear her?" The amulet

shrieked in our silent language. "You can have everything you desire!"

He grunted. "Oh, enough already."

The sword cleaved the amulet in two with one might strike. There was a blast of power unleashed in her destruction, and we were knocked across the chamber. Great billowing clouds of red smoke filled the room, and a familiar hacking cough came from somewhere.

"Oh, that was unpleasant," said Newt.

My witch and her familiar stepped from the fog. She stood naked, exposed in all her startling, supernatural beauty.

The Blade's warrior came into view, and he was struck dumb by what he saw. My witch took hold of the delicate strands of red fog and with a few snaps she shaped it into a long crimson robe she threw over her shoulders. With a sweep of her hand, she created a red hat to cover her head. It was a bit big, but I suspected that was on purpose.

"By the gods," said the warrior, "you are the most beautiful creature I have ever seen."

"Can I kill him now?" asked Newt.

My witch only smiled slyly as I floated into her hand.

"Very nicely done, my dear."

"Ah, there you are!" The warrior picked up the Willful Blade. The sword sighed. "I suppose it's too late to change my mind."

His bearer noticed the blood on the Blade. "What's this? We'll have to get you cleaned up, won't we? What have you been getting into?"

The fog slowly dissolved, and the chamber was crowded with a few dozen creatures, all of them freed victims of the amulet's stealing mists. The mists had spread throughout the fortress, and there were hundreds more scattered throughout. They were naked, but the element of surprise worked to their advantage. They quickly overwhelmed the warlord's forces. It helped that their leader was dead. Soldiers tended to lose their sense of purpose without someone to tell them what to do.

My witch left the fortress behind. The warrior trailed along with her for some time more. I suspected, having seen her true beauty, he was hoping to gain her favors. He didn't know the high price such favors might cost him, and because of her self-control, he never would.

"A rousing adventure," said the warrior. "We make an excellent team, witch."

"What did they do?" asked the Willful Blade.

"Oh, let him have his moment," I said.

As for my witch, I didn't know if she'd known all along this was the way it would go or if she'd only been fortunate enough to have a broom she could rely on. Like any good witch, mine was so mysterious, even I, her trusted broom, couldn't know for sure.

"I'm sorry for nearly destroying you," said the Blade.

"Think nothing of it. I knew you'd come to your senses sooner or later. It wasn't in your nature. Not truly."

"That was an awfully big chance to take," he said.

"Not so big. If you were as bloodthirsty as the amulet thought, you'd have killed your bearer a long time ago."

The Willful Blade shook with such laughter that he nearly fell out of his scabbard.

GREYBACK IN BLUE

The Automatic Detective

Like Penelope, Joseph Jung the mutant gorilla detective was top of my list of characters I'd love to put at the center of a story. A tough guy ape with the soul of a poet was made to order in this noir-ish tale of romance and all the dangers that go with falling for the wrong woman. We're all suckers when it comes to that special someone, and if a detective doesn't make bad decisions when his heart is involved, he's not much of a detective at all, if you ask me.

She lumbered into the office like an angel in blue born of the primeval wilds. There was a grace to her lope, like she was dancing on a cloud. Her fur shimmered like the sun on a good day, and she had the kind of haunches that might inspire more dimwitted apes to start caving in skulls, just on the off chance something like that might impress her.

She took off her hat with two fresh red roses pinned to it. I could smell them from here. I could smell her.

She batted her beady brown eyes at me and smiled. It was right then I knew I'd walk to the ends of the earth for this lady. I'd always been a haunches kind of primate.

Eve, my auto secretary, said, "Ms. Darrow is here to see Mack, but I said he was out on a case. Said maybe she should talk to you."

Darrow scratched something on a chalkboard in her hand and held it up for Eve to see. Thank you.

"No problem, sweetie. I'll leave you two alone." Eve said it like we were about to tear each other's clothes off and go at it like the wild beasts we once had been. Or maybe that was just my imagination. She rolled out of my office, closing the door behind her.

"What can I do for you, miss . . . . ?"

I let the question hang there, expecting she'd answer before too long. She put her little chalkboard in her purse and pursed her wide gray lips. "I was hoping to meet with your partner."

Only she didn't speak the words aloud. She beamed them telepathically into my brain, and I didn't get the impression she could actually talk. Mutation was a funny thing. It didn't always work out, but having telepathy when you couldn't speak seemed like a lucky break. She must've carried the chalkboard to talk with robots.

"He's out," I replied.

Mack, my bot partner, was popular in the way that only a seven foot tall titan of automation could be in this city.

Nobody gave much thought to a talking gorilla, though last time I'd checked, there weren't a lot of us dragging our knuckles across Empire's streets. It wasn't as if there was an official census, but you'd think someone would've been polite enough to alert me when another came along.

"Oh, I see," she said "I'm sorry to have bothered you."

She turned, and I leaned forward on my desk. "Maybe I could be of help."

She stopped. "Perhaps, though this problem of mine would be better solved by a robot."

The downside of being partnered up with an indestructible robot is that I, the four hundred pound gorilla, ended up being the little guy.

"I might not be able to throw a skimmer, miss, but I can take care of myself, just fine." I tapped my temple. "My partner is great for crushing nefarious individuals, but I'm the brains of this operation."

Eve piped up from the intercom. "He's a real gentle giant."

"Thank you, Eve," I said. "That'll be all."

She had a bad habit of listening in on private conversations. I'd have fiddled with her discretion index myself, but Mack, being a robot and sensitive about mucking around with other robots' programming, wouldn't allow it.

I flicked it off. I didn't know why I bothered. I was fairly certain Eve could override me. For all I knew the switch wasn't connected to anything other than that little red light under it, and I was only trapped in some elaborate psychological experiment. It didn't bother me though I would've liked it a lot more if a donut popped out of my desk when I responded properly.

Darrow smiled, though it was mostly in the eyes because she didn't have the capacity for such subtle expressions.

"Perhaps you could be of service."

I leaned back in my chair and tried to act casual. Drummed my toes on the desk as if I couldn't care less whether the only intelligent, female gorilla I'd ever met (who I hadn't even known existed until two minutes ago) walked out that door. In the jungle, I'd have beaten my chest and roared my intentions toward her, or so I assumed. The old instincts weren't what they used to be since I'd gotten smarter. Not that it mattered. The old rules didn't apply to we mutated apes. We were a more civilized breed.

By we, I meant the two of us in this room. Probably the only two on this whole planet.

You could say I was invested in getting to know her better.

"Why don't we start at the beginning, Ms. Darrow?"

I didn't ask where the name came from. She might have picked it using a phone book, like I had, or she might have had personal reasons for it. That was the upside about waking up as sentient one day. You got to define yourself however you liked.

"I need an item retrieved, Mr. Jung," she said.

"Please, call me Joseph. Or Joe, if you prefer."

Her eyes smiled again. It was absurd, but I was falling for this lady fast. Instinct demanded it, and who was I to argue with instinct?

My mutation did allow me the subtler expressions, and she must've spotted my discomfort with the vagueness of the request. It wasn't that I was against bending, or even breaking, some laws for this lady. Quite the opposite. I realized just how flexible my moral code had become at the moment.

"Oh, please, know it's nothing illegal," she said. "It's my property. I even know where it is. But I can't risk retrieving it myself. Rather, I'm not brave enough. I can't honestly say if it's dangerous or not, but I find my courage lacking."

"Nothing wrong with being afraid, Miss Darrow."

"You're very kind."

"What's this item, Miss Darrow?"

She snorted in a nervous way. "I was hoping to keep that confidential."

Normally, I'd have apologized for wasting her time and had Eve show her the door, but the thought of that lovely grayback in the blue dress lumbering out of my life wasn't something I considered.

"Go on." I leaned forward, tried to look thoughtful, as if I was still mulling this over.

"It's only an old heirloom. Something I inherited."

"Rich uncle?" I asked, only half-joking. If there was some undiscovered wealthy family of gorillas out there, I figured I should know about it.

She laughed. Verbally, it was a gruff snort, but telepathically, it was like an angel singing in my mind. "When I mutated, I was terribly alone. I'm sure you can relate."

I nodded.

"While I awaited citizen status, a human took me in. He helped with my adjustment period, and while he wasn't exceedingly wealthy, he had enough money to keep me comfortable for a very long time."

"Sounds like a swell guy."

My own transition had been a lot less pleasant. Once I'd proven my sentience, I'd been kicked out of the zoo, pushed into the mean streets, and told to fend for myself. It might've been a tragic story, but I'd made out all right so I guess I had nothing to gripe about. A conveniently dead wealthy uncle would've been nice to have though.

"He was," said Faye. "But he wasn't the most reputable sort of man. I had nothing to do with that part of his life. He very deliberately left me out of it. I suppose that's why he left me some money, perhaps as his way of making amends. And a chimp doll."

I remained neutral. "You're goofing."

"I suppose it sounds very silly to you, Mister . . . Joe. But in the early days of my sentience, that doll gave me a lot of comfort. It seemed something familiar in a frightening world."

It might have bothered my sensibilities, but I could see where she was coming from.

She removed a key from her purse and handed it to me.

"It opens a locker at the train station on Vanadium Street. I think he put it there because he assumed people would be watching his house."

She didn't elaborate on who those people might be or why they might be watching. I didn't ask because I didn't want to know.

"But you're afraid someone might be watching the locker too," I said.

"I know it's silly."

"Not at all. You're just taking precautions." I tucked the key in my pocket. "Why don't you wait here while I go have a look? Eve can make you some coffee or tea. Be back soon enough."

"Thank you, Joe. Thank you so very much."

I put a hand under her chin and smiled. "Just doing my job, Miss

Darrow."

"Please, Joe." She took my hand in hers and moved it to her lips. Her hot breath glided across my fingers. "Call me Faye."

I left her in my office. Eve caught me as I loped past her desk on my way to the front door.

"Hey, Romeo, you know she's lying to you, right?"

"You couldn't even hear her end of the conversation," I said.

"Didn't need to," said Eve. "Some women are trouble, and my body metric analyzer pings her as one of them."

"Didn't know you were programmed with ape metrics."

"Primates. They're all basically the same thing."

"I'll keep that in mind the next time you take offense when I compare you to a television. You never like the clientele."

"And I'm right seventy-four percent of the time," she said.

"It's a dirty business," I said. "What kind of sucker do you take me for? Of course, she's lying. Nobody walks through that front door unless they've got something to hide."

"But you're going anyway. Driven by your biological urge to impress her."

"It's a lonely world, and we don't all have the luxury of an off switch when the office closes." I grabbed my homburg off the coatrack. "Just see that she's comfortable. I'll be back in an hour."

I was out the door before she could say anything else I'd already figured out but didn't want to think about.

***

The Vanadium Street train station wasn't in the best neighborhood. A couple of young turks had staked out a street corner, scoping out vulnerable prey. I lumbered past, confident that they'd seek it elsewhere.

The station itself was in decent shape. Anything run by the city was kept up by state-of-the-art maintenance drones, so while the neighborhood might have had graffiti and garbage in the streets, that all stopped at the station's doors. It didn't keep the more ambitious vandals from trying, but biological ambition was no match for automated dedication. A drone was busy polishing the glass doors. It paused to open the door for me.

"Thanks," I said.

It beeped politely.

Foot traffic was heavy. The trains were how a lot of citizens got around this city, and they mostly ran on time, though there was always some new experimental prototype component ready to go on the fritz about twice a month. All just the sacrifice we citizens made in the pursuit of glorious technological innovation. Sometimes, it didn't seem like science marched on in Empire City so much as it was dragged kicking and screaming to places it wasn't ready to go where it would promptly cower in the corner or attack via industrial accident.

I didn't walk right to the locker but took my time to survey the station, looking for any suspicious sorts. There were plenty, but they were more of the pickpocket and petty criminal variety. The station had a reliable police presence that kept the more dangerous element outside. A cop and his auto partner stood by one wall, keeping an eye on things.

A dog had somehow gotten into the station. It wasn't threatening. Just weird. There weren't a lot of stray dogs in Empire City. Those that weren't captured by the animal control drones were usually caught in traffic or eaten by unspeakable mutated things that everyone knew were lurking in the sewers but pretended weren't there. The beagle wasn't big enough to be dangerous though.

Confident that I wasn't being followed or that if I had been, no one would be stupid enough to cause trouble here, I opened the locker. I wasn't sure what I'd find, but there was the monkey doll, just like Faye had said. It was a hell of an innocuous thing to be worried about.

Maybe she had been telling the truth.

"Do yourself a favor, friend," said someone behind me. "Walk away."

Except he hadn't said it. The voice was in my head. I could tell it came from behind somehow. Didn't know how, since it was a telepathic communication, but I didn't know the ins and outs of psychic mutation.

I turned, coming face-to-face with a chimpanzee in a sweater vest and bowtie.

"You gotta be kidding me," I said.

The crowd walked by, and no one paid either of us much attention. A couple of well-dressed primates wasn't that weird in this town.

"She's lying to you," beamed the chimp.

I didn't know why everyone kept telling me that.

"Give me the monkey, and forget you ever saw her," he said.

The beagle stepped out from among the commuters. "We don't want any trouble," he said.

Telepathic animals were crawling out of the woodwork, it seemed.

"Stay out of this, Gus," said the chimp. "I thought we agreed I'd handle this."

"Just thought you could use some backup," said Gus the dog. "This palooka's big. I think we should call in Jenny and Shawn."

I grabbed the monkey and tucked it under my arm. "Fellas, the monkey comes with me."

The beagle's eyes shimmered with a soft green sparkle, and I felt foreign thoughts creeping around in my head.

"What are you doing?" asked the chimp. "We aren't allowed to—"

"Stuff your code. This is too important," replied the dog as his eyes brightened, his mind pushed itself against mine. "Give us the monkey."

The pressure in my head felt like it might make my temples burst. My fingers loosened on the toy. My breath grew shorter as my throat tightened, and the base of my skull burned like someone was poking it with a red hot needle.

"You have a strong will," said the beagle, "but you will give it to—"

Something in my brain snapped. I'd lost most of the old instincts with my rise to sentience, and those that I still had I'd learned to suppress. His prodding must've broken some dam holding everything back. A dam I didn't even know I had until it sprung a leak.

I rose up and howled, beating my chest. Before I'd realized what I'd done, I pounced on the dog and hurled him into the lockers. He slumped on the floor with a sharp whine, and the pressure in my skull dissipated.

I turned on the chimp and smashed the cheap tile on either side of him. It cracked.

The chimp held his ground, though he didn't attack me. Nor did he try getting into my head.

"Give me the monkey, please."

My savagery subsided enough that I could see what was going on. A couple of intelligent primates chatting might not have drawn much attention, but a slavering, wild ape was a different story. The crowd had moved away. The cop and his auto were already on the way over.

The sensible part of me said to stay put and let the police sort this mess out. But another part of me said it was time to beat it. I turned and dashed for the exit. The pedestrians parted like the Red Sea, and I was outside in a flash. From there, it was only a short dash to my skimmer. Or it would've been if not for the lion and rhino standing in my way.

"Drop it," beamed the lion.

The cop and the auto stepped behind me. The cop had his ray gun out, but he wasn't sure where to point it.

"Jenny, keep them occupied," ordered the lion, who I assumed was Shawn.

The rhinoceros smashed a parked gyropod to one side and charged the cop. His heater scorched her thick hide, but it wasn't made to stop something that big. He dove away at the last moment, though his partner wasn't so lucky. Jenny crushed the poor auto underfoot.

The lion dove at me, but I got a lucky punch under his chin. While he was staggered, I grabbed him by the mane and smacked him a few more times across the nose. We danced around, but he outweighed me by a good hundred pounds. He nearly snapped my hand off in his jaws, and finally I was forced to push him away rather than be dragged under him, someplace I'd rather not have ended up.

I could feel him digging around in my brain with his telepathic claws. It was only adrenalin and instinct that kept him at bay.

I dredged up those instincts, but lions and apes don't grapple in the wild, despite what Tarzan pictures might say. Shawn coiled to spring as I went for my raygun, tucked in the holster under my jacket. I might have been faster, but I didn't need it often. Being a gorilla was usually enough.

Too slow, I was underneath the lion. His claws dug into my shoulders, and his jaws would've snapped around my throat if I hadn't rolled and used his momentum to fling him onward. He twisted and landed on his feet, sprang again. I had my heater out and blasted him point blank. The ray burned a hole in his shoulder, and he yowled, tumbling on the weakened leg. He limped forward, but with a wound, he wasn't quite so eager to test his speed again.

I scooped up the monkey doll off the street.

Jenny had crushed the police auto, but the cop she'd mesmerized stood there, staring blankly. She snorted and stomped the street with her foot.

The chimp in a bowtie emerged from the crowd. "No. You might hurt the monkey."

"I'll be careful," she said.

"No. Your help has only made this situation worse." The chimp held out his hand. "Mr. Jung, we need that monkey. It is rightfully ours. I know you're not in your right mind now. Your head is clouded. If you'll permit me to help you to see things correctly . . . ."

"Fat chance, Cheetah. If you think I'm going to let you muck about in my head, you're daffier than you look."

The sounds of sirens were closing in fast. I had to get out of here. Before these Jungle Jim rejects had another chance to mess with my mind. Before the cops showed.

I walked to my skimmer, never turning my back on the animals, avoiding looking them in the eyes, fearing they might pop something loose in my head that I might not be able to tie back down. They didn't make any move to stop me. They poked at my subconscious, but I was able to keep them locked out. At one point my vision blurred and I lost sight of the chimp before spotting him having taken up a safer position behind the lion.

I jumped into my skimmer and pulled out of there just as the police hovercraft started lighting up the sky. I got away with some luck, and with a little more luck, the animal gang would be too busy with the cops to follow.

***

I had a headache by the time I got back to the office. The kind that could only be fixed with a stiff drink and a bag of leaves to munch on.

Maybe after I gave Faye the monkey, she'd care to join me.

I kept my hand on the monkey the whole ride over there, not willing to even put the damned thing in the seat beside me. It was too precious to let go of. Even for a moment. The gashes and scrapes I'd gotten from the lion hurt, but it'd all be worth it in the end when I dropped this monkey in Faye Darrow's beautiful gray paws.

None of this was over, I figured. The telepathic animals knew who I was, and they'd definitely come looking for me. One problem at a time, and I knew what mattered most to me.

I pushed open the office door. Faye Darrow sat on the couch in the waiting area, sipping a tea.

"Oh, hello, Joe."

Eve sat behind her desk. She wasn't on. I could tell because she hadn't given me any sass yet.

"What happened to her?" I asked.

"I thought it best to switch her off." Faye nodded to a small device on the coffee table. "A wonderful little tool for shutting down robots. Very handy."

Things weren't adding up. They hadn't been since Faye Darrow had first walked into my office. I'd told myself I didn't care, but now, I was beginning to think maybe I did.

Her eyes flashed as she tightened a telepathic vice around my instincts. I couldn't think clearly, but I could think enough to see that she was manipulating me. She had from the beginning. Little pokes and prods to my inner ape. Nothing obvious. Just a subtle push to the animalistic drive to impress females. A drive that had been buried too long and was all-too-eager to come out.

"I see you succeeded," she said. "I'll admit to some doubt the others might compromise you. That's why I wanted the robot on this. Biological minds can be so unpredictable. But then I realized how much easier it would be to convince you, and thought it worth a shot."

She set down her cup of tea and smiled at me with her burning green eyes. Even as I knew it was stupid, I knew I'd wrestle a thousand lions for her approval.

"Oh, dear, Joe," she beamed. "You're a mess. I do hope you know how much I appreciate your help. And your pain will be over soon enough." She caressed my cheek and took the monkey from me.

Except I wouldn't let it go.

The smartest thing in the world would've been to pull my raygun out and blast her. I couldn't do that. It wasn't just her grip on my mind. For better or worse, she was the only mutant gorilla I'd run across, and I couldn't just let her slip away.

But I didn't have to give her the damn monkey either.

She tugged harder. "Joe, honey, don't be stubborn about this."

"What's in the doll?" I asked.

"That's none of your affair, dear."

She abandoned all telepathic subtlety and stomped around in my head with sudden, overwhelming force. I screamed, fell on my face, drooling. My body felt like jelly held together by my suit, and my vision blurred.

But I didn't let go of that damn monkey.

"Have it your way. I was going to do this anyway, but I was hoping to make it more pleasant." She rolled me to one side and reached under my jacket for my gun. I couldn't make a move to stop her.

Without warning, the pressure in my head lessened, and my body was mine again. I grabbed her wrist and squeezed. The pain disrupted her concentration, and more of my own will struggled against her cage. I pushed her away, drew my heater. I couldn't bring myself to point it at her.

"What's in the monkey, Faye?" I asked.

"The future," beamed the telepathic chimp from behind me. "Our future."

I realized then that he'd been there all along. I hadn't left him at the train station. He'd telepathically blurred my perceptions. I'd known he was there, but I hadn't known too. It was why I hadn't let go of the monkey in the skimmer. If all the animals could do that, it also explained how a lion and a rhino could walk around without causing a scene though you'd think robots would notice. Then again, this was Empire. If a wild animal walked around with enough nonchalance, nobody much cared.

"Not your future," said Faye. "You have no future."

The chimp shook his head. "You have to let it go. We can't keep fighting this war. It doesn't' matter anymore. This is a new world. We can move on."

She growled and beat the floor with her fists. "Kill him for me, Joe."

She flipped some switches, letting loose some of my more uncivilized instincts. He threw up a wall around those instincts. My mind was a battleground between these two, and I was only along for the ride.

"The monkey has an element in it, not found on your world," he said. "My people, we need it to reproduce."

"Your people?" I asked. "You're Pilgrims? There's a race of space chimps and alien gorillas and nobody bothered to tell me?"

"It's more complex than that," he said. "This isn't my body. It's only borrowed. Just as hers is. Just as the others. We are, for lack of time for a better explanation, extraterrestrial symbiotes that find hosts with lower creatures."

He passed a mental snapshot in my mind of a green worm, long and thin, wrapped around a spinal column. Gorilla, lion, chimp, rhino. It all worked the same. It wasn't a pretty picture, and Faye Darrow went from the gorilla of my dreams to a thing out of a horror picture.

"We only want to live in peace," said the chimp. "Most of us anyway. But others, they still want to fight the old wars. They want to take our most sacred right and use it as a weapon."

"He's lying, Joe," she said. "He's manipulating you, trying to trick you. Give the monkey to me, kill him, and we can be together. Does it matter if I borrowed this body? You can still have it. You can still have me."

She pushed harder, and I pointed the raygun at the chimp.

He said, "You're stronger than this, Joseph Jung."

He shored up my mind, and while I wasn't thinking clearly, I got the big picture. Faye Darrow was pushing me to kill. The chimp was leaving the choice up to me.

I blasted someone. In the moment, I wasn't at all certain who it was, but someone was going to get shot, and at the time, I wasn't sure if I cared who it was just so long as the pressure in my head eased up.

My hand was shaking, and my vision was blurry, but I had managed to burn a hole in Darrow's side and her pretty blue dress.

Her concentration slipped, and I felt like myself again. Maybe for the first time since meeting her.

Those eyes, they pleaded with me. They were beautiful, all right, but behind them, I could see the hints of a fresh telepathic push.

"Joe, please."

I decked her. Not my proudest moment, but there was nothing else I could do short of shooting her. She fell flat with a groan.

"Joe, you idiot." Her choppy telepathic words were like distant static as the chimp locked down her telepathic mojo. "You could've had it all."

"Sorry, beautiful," I said. "Even if I believed you, some things just aren't worth the price."

***

Faye's borrowed body, a greyback named Grapefruit, didn't die. They patched her up, put her in the zoo. I only went to see her once.

I hated the zoo.

Grapefruit sat among the other gorillas in the enclosure, and I pondered what I'd lost when I'd mutated. Zoo life wasn't the bee's knees, but there were times when it didn't look so bad from this side of the enclosure.

Denham the chimp walked up beside me. "She's adjusting well. She should make a full recovery."

"Something positive," I said. I didn't know if I could've lived with myself if I'd killed her, but in a way, I had. Faye Darrow had been two entities, and divided, neither of them had much use for me.

"You did the right thing, Mr. Jung," said Denham

"What about Faye?" I asked.

"Extraction from the host is never without damage to us, but she is recovering and we are hoping to rehabilitate her." He shrugged. "But I fear some can never move beyond old wounds."

"We've all got our scars." I ran my hand across the fresh ones I sported from this affair. "You don't happen to have any other gorilla alien hybrids among you, do you?"

Denham chuckled. "Sorry. But when we do, you'll be the first to know."

I smiled. In a city where superscience ran amok, tomorrow was a place of infinite possibilities. Most of those possibilities were dangerous misfires, but even among the worst Empire had to offer, there was always hope.

"Let's get out of here." I cast one last look at Grapefruit. "I hate this place."

"Can I buy you a beer, Mr. Jung? It's the least I can do for you, all things considered."

"You're right." I slapped Denham on his shoulder. "It is the least you could do."

He might not have been the primate I'd planned on sharing a drink with at the end of the week, but all things considered, he wasn't such a bad guy. Sometimes, you took what you could get and were grateful to get it.

DEATH, DUST, AND OTHER INCONVENIENCES

Too Many Curses

Too Many Curses *is easily my most fairy tale like story and probably my most neglected. It's not as flashy as most of my other stories, and the premise doesn't jump out at you. Maybe that's why I like it as much as I do. Telling stories about tough-as-nails werewolves and super genius space squids is relatively easy. Those types of characters are made to be heroes, but Nessy and the denizens of Margle's cursed castle are exactly everything we wouldn't expect heroes to be. Somehow, despite that, they get by. Here's a story where they do just that.*

A shadow of death stalked the halls of Margle's castle.

Nessy found out about this from Humbert the hummingbird, who heard it from Richard the staircases ghost, who was told of the shadow's presence by Bethany the banshee, who had met the shadow in that place between life and death where ghosts spent a lot of their time.

It wasn't the first time one of death's shadows had visited the castle. Death often came calling on wizards, and any wizard of any accomplishment had ways of dealing with such shadows. But Margle was dead, and his castle was without any defense against the grim specter that now roamed, invisibly, waiting to strike.

"We have to do something," said Sir Thedeus, the former knight, now small fruit bat, sitting on Nessy's shoulder.

She petted the nurgax, her purple pet. It didn't do much, but it had saved her life at least once, and it was devoted to a fault. "What would you have me do? It's death. Best to ignore it."

"Ye canna ignore death, lass," he replied.

"Weren't you a warrior once?" she asked.

"Aye."

"Wasn't it your job to ignore death then? Or did you rush onto the battlefield assuming she wasn't there?"

"It's an excellent point," said Echo, the bodiless voice.

"Death is different for a warrior," said Thedeus. "We have no recourse against it, but surely Margle has a trick or two at his disposal."

"I suppose it couldn't hurt to talk to the shadow," said Nessy. "See what it wants."

"Ye can do that?" asked Thedeus.

Since inheriting the castle from her not-quite-dead-but-close-enough master, Nessy had been learning the art of magic from Margle's brother, who unlived as a pair of eyeballs, some teeth, and a bit of brain in a jar.

Yazbip thought she had some talent for it, but her studies had been hampered by the physical limitations of her teacher as well as all her daily duties. She understood now why wizards kept people around to tidy things up. Not that she was interested in giving up her job. She found more satisfaction in a dusted hallway than in learning to levitate.

"It's a smidge beyond my talents," she said. "But I'm sure we can find something in Margle's collection to enable it."

"Is that a good idea?" asked Echo. "Maybe we should just leave it alone."

Nessy's pragmatic nature agreed. She had enough to worry about without adding a personification of death to that list. But she was also not the kind to allow a problem to fester when it might be solved easily. In the end, it was Yazbip who convinced her, assuring her that while it was unlikely to accomplish much, it wasn't likely to make things worse.

Nessy, Echo, Sir Thedeus, Yazbip the Magnificent, and the nurgax gathered in the garden room and prepared to summon the shadow to have a chat. Margle's garden was filled with all manner of exotic, deadly plant life, but as long as one was cautious enough to avoid the carnivorous chrysanthemums and ignored the whispered promises of the wishing tree (whose cursed wishes acted as its means of reproduction, always ending with the wisher becoming a wishing tree themselves), the garden was a lovely place and one of Nessy's favorite rooms.

"This should do nicely," said Yazbip as Nessy levitated him behind her.

"Should'nah we do this in a tomb?" asked Thedeus.

Yazbip chuckled, sending bubbles to the surface of the yellow fluid he floated in. "Hardly. You're unlikely to find death anywhere near a tomb. Everyone there is already dead. Death's business is among the living."

A tendril of vines dragged a mouse out of a crack in the wall and pulled it into the dirt. Nessy was certain it was a normal mouse. All the castle residents cursed into mouse shape knew enough to avoid this room.

"See?" Yazbip's teeth floated in a smug grin. "Death and life go side by side."

A nearby purple and red flower of generous size waved its hungry petals in Sir Thedeus's direction. He clung tighter to Nessy's shoulder. With Yazbip's guidance, Nessy drew a circle with several runes. It wasn't all that difficult because it was relatively simple magic. It wasn't an attempt to compel the shadow, but to merely coax him into appearing. The choice was entirely his, and appear, he did.

The shadow of death was a tall, handsome figure with a dark face, black eyes, wrapped in a billowing pale cloak. He stood there quietly surveying the gathering. There was knowledge in his eyes. The knowledge most mortals spent a lifetime ignoring.

"Should we say something?" asked Echo.

"Hello," said Nessy.

The shadow turned his gaze upon her and smiled. "Hello, Nessy."

"You know me?" she asked.

"We are acquainted, are we not?" he replied. "I remember all the souls that were once mine, however briefly. A kobold soul is all the more unique among that number."

Sir Thedeus flew down to land before Nessy. "If ye've come for the lass, ye'll have to get through me first."

The nurgax joined his side. It growled at the shadow.

"If I'd come for her, she would already be mine," said the shadow of death.

"If not for Nessy, who have you come for?" asked Echo. "Margle?"

The shadow frowned. "Alas, his soul remains beyond my reach for the moment. But I can afford to be patient. No, I'm only here as an observer for the moment. It has been perhaps too long since any interesting demises in this place. There is a balance to this universe, and Death herself sent me to see if everything was in order."

He smiled again, and the carnivorous chrysanthemums folded into themselves. Hungry vines retracted into the ground.

"If I should deem it necessary, I, as her authorized agent, shall correct that. But there are so many interesting souls to be found here that I must admit I'm having a bit of trouble with my selection."

"Ach, have we nah enough troubles without ye here, poking about?" asked Thedeus. "Since when does death feel the need to make house calls anyway?"

"You're upset. I can understand that. It is your nature to fear me, but rest assured, I only do as my mistress demands."

The shadow faded.

"Get back here, ye coward!" shouted Thedeus. "I'll send ye back to yer mistress with a story to tell!"

But the shadow didn't return.

"What are we going to do, lass?" asked Thedeus.

"What can we do?" Nessy replied as she started scrubbing away the chalk. "It's death. We can only wait and hope for the best."

***

Sir Thedeus had never been the hopeful type. Hope had always seemed the last refuge of the powerless, and under normal circumstances, he would've agreed that there wasn't much they could do against Death herself.

But Margle had cheated death, in a fashion, and Nessy had escaped her grim clutches. Among the castle's cursed artifacts, there must have been something to deal with a shadow of death, and he resolved to find it. He dug through one of the many magical laboratories. It was organized in a way that only a mad wizard could understand. Swords and potions and enchanted amulets lay strewn about on tables and shelves.

He struggled with a shimmering battle axe that he couldn't lift.

"I don't think Nessy would like us doing this," said Echo.

"The lass is too practical for her own good." he replied. "She has enough to deal with already. We'll take care of this problem ourselves. Now help me."

"I don't have a body."

"Ye have eyes, don't ye?"

"Actually, no."

"Well, ye can still see, can't ye?" He put his ear to a blue potion. Something inside the stopped clay vial growled. "How do ye see anyway?"

"Ask Margle. What are we looking for?"

"Yazbip says it'll be a twisted staff, likely made of bone, with a white gemstone set on top."

"Yazbip is advising you? There's no way this can go horribly wrong then."

"He's a capable wizard."

"Since when do you believe that?"

"Since he agreed to help me put death in its place. Now quit yapping and help me find it."

Echo sighed. "This is against my better judgment, but I think it's over here."

Thedeus perked up. "Where, lass?"

She whistled until he could find her. "Aha, that must be it." He clambered up the staff gleefully.

"I don't know. That gem is yellow, not white. And the staff is made of wood."

"Ach, 'tis close enough."

He undid the clasp on the scroll tied to his body and unfurled the document. "Now all we have to do is say the magic words, and it should draw death's shadow right into it."

"Won't she just send another?"

"Then we'll capture that one too," he said. "And the one after that. And the one after that. We'll capture all her shadows if we have to."

"This is a really bad idea."

"Have some optimism, Echo lass. Even if it dunna work, it canna make things worse."

Thedeus perched atop the red diamond and read the incantation aloud. As he read, the gem warmed under his feet and leaves sprouted from the staff. Echo thought of interrupting, but often interrupted magic was the worst kind.

Robots Versus Slime Monsters

A warm wind howled through the laboratory, and Sir Thedeus's voice boomed in thunderous cadence. He dropped the parchment but kept reading. The blank expression on his face confirmed that the magic had taken control.

The hot air burned Echo. She didn't know if it was the magical nature of it or her lack of a body, but it felt like her mind was burning around the edges. She screamed as the not-quite-pain nibbled at her exposed being.

It faded away. Sir Thedeus stopped incanting. He blinked himself alert.

"How are you?" she asked.

"Perfectly fine." He tapped the cold gem under him. "Do ye think it's in there now?"

"It can't be that easy."

"Optimism, lass."

Cracks appeared in the gem as it leaked plumes of green smoke in the air. Thedeus flew to a table on the opposite end of the room. The gem shattered into dust, and the staff grew larger and leafier. It sprouted two legs, a twisted wooden arm, and a head with tangled vines for hair. The rasping vaguely feminine figure fell to one knee.

"Is that a dryad?" asked Echo.

"Another of Margle's cursed prisoners," said Thedeus. "If nothing else, at least we've freed her."

The dryad put her hand on a table and pushed herself to her feet. Grass and flowers sprouted from the table where she stood.

"Easy now," said Thedeus. "Yer free now."

The dryad stared at him with the empty knots where eyes should be. Half-laughing, half-shrieking, she ran from the room, knocking over tables and potions in her mad, aimless dash. Everything she touched sprouted thick grass and strange flowers, and even after she'd disappeared (though her shrieking could still be heard), the greenery continued to grow up the walls and all over everything like a ravenous emerald hunger.

Echo said, "I think we just made it worse."

***

Sir Thedeus flew after the crazed dryad. She wasn't hard to find. The castle's echo made it difficult to locate the shrieking, but all the wild plants sprouting in her wake led the way.

"What are we going to do when we find her?" asked Echo. "Shouldn't we consult Yazbip?"

"There's no time," he said. "He'd probably only screw it up."

"I'm not sure he's the one to blame."

"Ye dinna need to blame yerself, Echo lass. Ye never claimed to know anything about magic."

She grumbled. "You're too kind, Thedeus."

They found the dryad in one of the smaller libraries. There were a half-dozen of the studies, containing the books Margle had deemed unimportant enough to not be in the main library. The one-armed dryad stood hunched in the middle of the room. She wheezed as leaves fell off her body. Her graying bark peeled away.

The firefly in a jar on one of the shelves said, "Most interesting."

Thedeus ignored the firefly, a powerful demon in cursed form. Actually, hundreds of fireflies spread throughout the castle.

"I don't think she's feeling well," said Echo. "Is she dying?"

"She's not truly alive in the first place," answered the firefly unbidden. "Dryads sometimes shed their limbs and enterprising wizards will sometimes transform those into magical staffs. If the wrong magic should somehow come in contact with the staff, it'll take on a semblance of life, but it's only a semblance. It never lasts long."

The dryad collapsed and fell silent, unmoving.

"Well, that takes care of that problem then," said Thedeus.

"Oh yes," said the firefly. "I assume you have someone fetching the death orchid now."

"Ah, yes, the orchid," said Sir Thedeus. "I'm sure there's one around here someplace."

"Don't tell me you forgot the death orchid."

"We dinna expect this to happen."

"We weren't prepared," said Echo.

The grass and flowers continued to sprout, covering the dryad and the floor in a mossy overgrowth.

The demon firefly chuckled. That could only be an ill omen.

"Oh, well, then. In that case, you should probably run along before she . . . oh, my. That was faster than I expected."

The mound split open as four mrigendra, crosses between a ferocious feline and mandrake root, spilled out. Their bodies were lumpy and covered in dirt and roots. One had a mane made of grass. They raised their heads and shrieked with an earsplitting wail.

One of the lionesses sniffed the firefly's jar, but she flared the wicked fire on her tail. It backed away, growling.

"They're no danger to me or the bodiless one," she said, "but I can't say the same for you, bat."

The creatures eyed Sir Thedeus. They licked their mouths with the thorny vines of their tongues. He flew from the room, and the growling beasts gave chase.

"How do we stop them?" asked Echo.

"Why should I tell you?" said the demon.

The study was covered in creeping plants, spreading to every surface.

"Because if you don't, the castle could fall into disaster."

The grass growing on the desk curled around the edges of the demon's jar but shied away from covering her. "I rather like disasters. It's in my nature."

"But if this castle is overrun with plants, who will you torment? The daffodils?"

The demon bobbed. "That is an excellent point. Would get rather dreary after a while. Still, I can't just tell you how to fix this. That's also against my nature. Oh, I know it's inconvenient, but we must bargain."

"You can't have my soul."

The firefly flew in clockwise circles. "Why does everyone assume their soul is so valuable? There are billions of souls out there. What's so special about yours?"

"What do you want then?" asked Echo.

"Is it truly so difficult to guess? What do you, a bodiless poet, have to offer me? What is your only worthwhile possession in this world?"

"I can't agree to that," said Echo.

"Well then, I guess dreariness is our future unless Nessy, the clever girl, cleans up this mess. She's rather good at that."

Echo sighed. "Very well. But only if you promise me this'll work."

The demon laughed. "My dear, dear empty lady, if you can't trust a queen of the pits, who can you trust?"

***

The mrigendras chased Sir Thedeus through the castle, their horrible screeches filling the air. The lioness at the lead would spring with deadly grace and swipe within inches of swatting him from the air.

"That's it, ye great dull beasties!" he shouted. "Follow me to yer doom!"

With the monsters nipping at his wings, he led them. His worry that the mrigendras might get distracted by easier prey proved groundless as most of the residents of the castle were very good at hiding from the more terrible things that might lurk about. They had plenty of practice.

He flew into the bestiary. It wasn't his favorite place. He could tolerate the upper levels, where the less horrible things were caged. The menagerie of rare and magical creatures howled, hooted, and roared as Thedeus and the mrigendras continued their chase between the cages. Thedeus flew through the bars of his chosen cage, and perched atop the head of the monster within.

"Haha." He fluttered his pointed ears and smirked at the mrigendras snapping at the cage bars. "Dinna think ye could catch me that easy, did ye?"

The chimera under him shifted, but didn't wake from its nap.

"Ah, come on now. Get up, ye lazy abomination."

He nipped at its hairy lion head with his pointed teeth. It brushed at him with one paw as the snake that was its tail hissed in annoyance. The snake struck, but Thedeus nimbly flew aside, and the serpent buried its venomous fangs into the chimera's goat head. This shocked the dragon and lion heads awake, and all of them snarled at Thedeus who dove back and forth across the dragon's head. Its snapping jaws came dangerously close to swallowing him whole, but he was just a touch faster. The mrigendras strained against the cage, batting with their thorny paws as Thedeus played a dangerous game of dodge.

"Ye canna catch me, ye stupid beasts. Ye know what ye have to do."

The dragon exhaled a gout of fire. Thedeus swooped to safety, but the mrigendras went up like dry kindling. They ran around in shrieking panic, but the area around the chimera's cage was fire-proofed for obvious reasons. They burned into harmless piles of ash in very short order.

The chimera's goat head bleated at Sir Thedeus, who watched from a safe perch.

"Me thanks to ye, creature."

The monster roared once then curled up in its cage and went back to sleep.

Fortune the black cat, who had been lounging, undetected, in a shadowy crevice in the wall, said, "You shouldn't have done that. It's bad luck to burn mrigendras."

"Ah, I dunna believe in luck. Now if ye'll excuse me, I still have a shadow of death to deal with."

"This way," said Echo. "Quickly."

Dodger the weasel came scampering in behind her (or maybe in front of or beside her) with a packet of seeds tied around her back.

"I'm coming, I'm coming."

Thedeus flew down to Echo's general direction. "No need to worry, lasses. I've handled it."

"What did you do?" asked Echo.

"I solved the problem."

Echo groaned. "You burned them, didn't you?"

"T'was the simplest solution."

"You aren't supposed to burn them."

Fortune stretched. His long tail swished back and forth. "Told you."

"Do you still need these?" Dodger held up the seed pouch.

"I don't know. We were supposed to feed them to the mrigendras, and they'd become harmless."

"They canna get much more harmless than they are now," said Thedeus.

A breeze picked up some of the ashes as they swirled in miniature cyclones. The cyclones merged, growing larger and more powerful.

"Ye gods, I hate magic."

"Can we get Nessy now?" asked Echo before the wails of the eight foot tall ashen tornado became too loud to be heard over.

***

Nessy shouted the incantation over the howling whirlwinds. This was the third time she'd had to do it. The first time, she'd been too close, and they'd drowned her out. The second, she'd been too far away, and the spell hadn't found its target. This time, she was just right, and with the final magic syllable, the tornadoes lost all their energy. In their dying moment, they spewed ash, covering Nessy, the nurgax, Sir Thedeus, Dodger, the walls, ceiling, and floor with a layer of grime.

"Well done, Nessy lass." Thedeus, perched on her shoulder, coughed and sputtered.

"Yes, well done," agreed the demon firefly in her jar. Though it wasn't her voice she used, but Echo's. Borrowed for a few days as price for the knowledge of the seeds that hadn't done Echo any good. Echo herself could've been anywhere, but Nessy assumes the voiceless, bodiless poet was nearby.

"You should really have known better," said Nessy.

The nurgax shook the grime from its wings, and growled in a low and disappointed tone.

"Ach, we were just trying to help," said Thedeus.

"I didn't start it," said Dodger. "I'm just here because Echo needed someone to carry the seeds."

Fortune the cat, who had somehow managed to avoid getting covered in ash, licked his paw. "And I didn't do anything."

Sir Thedeus glanced at the mess that had been made. It seemed like half the castle was in disarray. Bits and pieces were strewn everywhere. A suit of armor had been knocked over, scattering into pieces. The beasts in the menagerie were still creating a racket that could be heard from halfway across the castle. A painting of a lake had fallen off its wall to lay upside down, its cursed resident up to his knees in water. Grass was continuing to grow out of many crevices in the brickwork.

"T'was not my greatest triumph," admitted Thedeus, "but it all worked out in the end."

"Yes, aside from the mess and the inconvenience and the fact that you didn't actually do anything about the shadow of death, I'd say it was a complete success," said the demon with a chuckle.

"I appreciate what you were trying to do," said Nessy, though it was a strain of even her near legendary good nature to keep from snarling a bit as she said it. "But next time, perhaps you should consult with me beforehand."

Thedeus grumbled to himself. It was as close to an apology as he would come.

Death's shadow came floating out of the darkness.

"Hello, Nessy," he said.

"We dinna summon you, shadow," said Thedeus.

"If I waited to be summoned, I'd be far less busy than I am."

Thedeus was about to say something else, when Nessy gently shushed him.

"Did you find what you were looking for?" she asked.

The shadow smiled inscrutably. "Indeed. I think after what I've seen today that you've no need of my special attentions. You earn your lives, every day, I see. But then again, doesn't everyone? But you have a castle to tend, and I should be on my way."

"Good day then," said Nessy.

The shadow pulled his pale cloak around himself and with a slight bow, he vanished.

"Did ye hear that?" asked Thedeus. "He left because of what we did. So in a way, we saved the day."

"In a very selective way," agreed the demon.

Nessy patted him on his head. "I suppose we can't argue with the results. Now help me tidy up this mess."

"Tis me pleasure, lass." He struggled to carry a gauntlet that was far too heavy for him, settling for dragging it noisily across the stone floor.

Nessy chuckled to herself before picking up the gauntlet and the bat while getting back to work.

WORK ETHIC

Monster

Not to spoil anything, but this story takes place before the novel it's based on. If you have read Monster, *you'd understand why. If you haven't read* Monster, *well, it won't much matter to you. The original novel was intended to be urban fantasy without the glamor or grit, just an everyday world where magic happened to be real. It's another common theme in my stories, but it's the central theme of the novel and continues into this short story.*

The divorce didn't bother Kristine. Mom and Dad had been at each other's throats for a year, and the only reason they'd stayed together as long as they had was due to a well-meaning but doomed effort for Kristine's sake. Whatever the hell that meant. It sucked being from a broken home, but it sucked worse having a home where everyone was always shouting about some stupid bullshit that wasn't what they were really mad about in the first place.

Worse, were all the glares. Even when her parents weren't talking to each other, they were always giving each other dirty looks and mumbling under their breath. They thought she didn't notice, but she did.

When they finally called it splits, it was a relief. She hated that they'd been so miserable for so long, and she hated that she was indirectly the cause of it.

She wasn't happy with the new situation, but at least it was a new kind of suck to deal with.

Dad motioned to his new house. "What do you think, Krissy?"

Kristine cringed. "Dad . . . ."

"Sorry. It's Kristine now. I forget."

"It's okay," she replied, both to his apology and the new house.

"I know this is tough," he said.

She nodded as he droned on. She hated it when her parents were understanding. He carried her bags into the house for her, saying stuff as he did so. She followed. The house was wholly unexceptional. Two stories and a basement. Not much furniture aside from the few pieces Dad had gotten in the settlement. Her bedroom was at least nice, though it only had an old dresser and a sleeping bag in it.

"I'll get you a new bed soon. But for now, it'll be like camping." He realized how dumb that sounded and frowned. "Look, Krissy, Kristine, I know this isn't easy for—"

"It's not easy for any of us, Dad. But it's better." She went to the window and parted the dusty old flower print curtains. The view was nothing more than the brick wall of the neighboring house.

He smiled. "Okay. Dinner's in an hour. Oh, and the cable or internet isn't hooked up yet. Sorry."

"Whatever." She grumbled. She despised when she sounded like a teenager. "I brought a book."

"That's good. And at least we still have electricity, right?" He flicked the light switch off and on. The bulb popped. The little bit of sunlight that could filter through the window cast the room in a gray darkness.

"Shit. Don't worry, honey, I'll change that."

"Whateve . . . I can change it. Where do you keep the bulbs?"

There weren't any. For dinner, Dad had planned his famous spaghetti, foiled by the realization that he didn't have a good pot for the pasta. A few other necessary supplies quickly popped up, and Dad made a run to the store. Kristine elected to stay home and read at the dining room table, where the only comfortable chairs were. She didn't listen to music like she normally did because the sounds of the house, creaks and mysterious pops, put her in the mood of a put upon fifteen year old in an unfair universe. Suitably melodramatic, she knew, but she indulged herself.

Rodents skittered in the walls. She ignored them until they started scratching rhythmically. One long scratch followed by two short scratches followed by two long scratches. The pattern repeated itself for a few minutes before she noticed.

She set down her book and put her ear to the wall.

The scratching stopped. When she turned back, her book had moved. It was halfway under the refrigerator and wiggling its way out of sight. She stepped on it, only afterward thinking it might be a rat or some other unpleasant creature stealing it.

She moved her foot. The book shimmied an inch deeper under the fridge. Kristine was almost finished with the book, and though it wasn't a very good story, she hadn't invested 312 pages of her life to watch the last forty get stolen by a rat. She yanked the book away, delicately but firmly.

A little blue creature clung to the book. Only a few inches tall and with a small, green-cheeked face, the humanoid stared into Kristine's face and smiled sheepishly. The pixie dropped to the floor and zipped under the refrigerator.

Kristine knew there were such things as faeries. She'd always known. But she'd also learned at thirteen that the part of the brain that allowed people to acknowledge such things atrophied. She was an exception. She'd passed an aptitude test last year when she'd been shown a small dragon in a cage. She'd spent an afternoon in a special class where she, along with two other students, were told they were magically cognizant children born to incognizant parents. It was a rare thing, but it happened.

She'd already figured it out on her own when her parents were oblivious to the weird creatures they refused to acknowledge. It was relief to learn there was an explanation for it. When Dad came home, she thought about telling him about the pixie, but he wouldn't get it. The counselor told her there was no point in trying to talk to normal people about stuff like this.

She stayed up the first night in the house, tucked in her uncomfortable sleeping bag, armed with a flashlight, listening to every little noise. She didn't spot one pixie, and all she did was deprive herself of sleep.

The next day, she had Dad take her to the library, where she checked out some books on faeries, and, after a short nap, read up on what to expect. Dad was just happy she was engaged. After they went to bed, she decided to try an experiment.

She found a pair of Dad's old shoes, used some sandpaper to scuff them, and put them in the kitchen, along with a slice of bread and several grapes. When she woke up the next day, the shoes were shined, and the food was gone.

The pixies made her life a lot easier. All her chores were taken care of by her new faerie workforce. She rarely caught a glimpse of them, and those glimpses were fleeting. But they were there. In the walls. Taking care of stuff. They proved more adept than she would've imagined, hooking up the cable, assembling furniture, and fixing some loose, leaky pipes. And they worked cheap, for cookies or half-a-sandwich. She'd once given them a Big Mac, and they'd cleaned the whole house, spotless, top-to-bottom.

"I really appreciate how much you've been helping out around here," said Dad one afternoon.

"Happy to help." She liked the faeries, liked having a secret that she didn't have to feel guilty about because Dad couldn't understand even if she had told him. He still blamed the scratching in the walls on rats.

He kissed the top of her head. "It's good to see you smile again, Kristine. Things are going to be all right."

She nodded. "Things are going to be just fine, Dad."

Things started not being fine three weeks later.

She was awoken one night by the shaking of her bed. She turned on the lamp by the end table, and expected the faeries to flee like they always did. But seven of the little blue creatures perched at the foot of her bed.

She avoided any sudden movements as her eyes adjusted.

"Hey, girls."

Two of the faeries carried her iPhone between them. They dropped it on the mattress and chirped.

Slowly, she took it. The faeries jumped back while chattering.

"Thanks, I guess."

They squealed curiously.

"What? You want something for this? It's mine. You don't get food for bringing me something that's mine."

The creatures flapped their butterfly wings, flying in small circles. They squeaked sweetly.

"No."

The pixies chirped among themselves before flying away into a vent. Kristine rolled over to go to sleep. A leg of her bed snapped off and jarred her awake.

Dad inspected the damage. "Nothing serious. Just a loose screw. I can fix it."

Kristine imagined she could hear the pixies chuckling in the dark vent. "Guess you get what you pay for," she mumbled to herself. She'd given them a potato and a pudding cup to but her bed together.

In the morning, Dad informed her that the shower wasn't working.

"Pipe must be clogged," he said. "I'll get someone to take a look at it."

After he'd left for work, she addressed the house. "Okay, I get it. You're having a little fun, but enough is enough." A cupboard door broke off as she opened it, and Kristine gritted her teeth. "Very funny, girls."

Dozens of faeries perched atop the refrigerator and along the countertops.

"Okay, I shouldn't really do this, but just this once. But only if you promise to fix everything."

The pixies danced around, whistling sweetly, as she gave each of them a Cheerio. They thanked her by cheerfully whistling as they disappeared into the darkened corners they called home.

"Enjoy them, but just fix it," said Kristine.

They kept their side of the deal, repairing everything when she wasn't looking. She started feeding them more regularly, even when they didn't do anything, and things were fine again.

Until a month later when they stopped being fine again.

She awoke in the middle of the night when her bed came crashing apart. She turned on her lamp to glimpse hundreds of pixies flying around in her room.

She rubbed her head where a part of the frame had smacked her.

A pixie settled in her hand and chirped. It gently nipped her fingertip. She shook it off.

"If you think I'm going to pay you—"

A picture frame fell off her wall and broke. It had belonged to her grandmother, who had died before Kristine had met her.

"You little bastards. That's it. No more food then."

The pixies unleashed a cacophony of off-key chimes and chirps.

"I said no more!"

They scattered in all directions, and Kristine went to tell Dad what had happened. He might remember long enough to help her figure things out.

Dad was in his room, dancing around in wild circles, laughing and singing nonsensically. When she tried to stop him, he nearly smacked her in the face with one of his flailing arms. Manic delight swirled in his eyes as he twirled.

The lights went out, and the house became quiet. Faeries skittered around in the darkness. Downstairs, something broke. Loudly. It sounded like dishes were being shattered.

Kristine swept her phone across the hall to see the dozens of little blue creatures in the hall.

She shut the door. Dad's crazy dance occupied the center of the room, so she flattened herself against the wall. She dialed 911. The operator didn't call her a nut, but she was also told this was the wrong number for crazed pixies. They transferred her to a different department, where someone took her report again and got her address.

Dad continued to dance, though his energy flagged, and it became more of a limp trot. The pixies didn't come into the room, but she could hear them breaking stuff in the house. It was thirty minutes later when she heard another human voice. She ventured out into the dark while all around her the pixies flittered.

A guy at the bottom of the stairs shined a flashlight in her face. "Are you the one who called for crypto containment?"

She covered her eyes from the light. "Yeah. That's me. Are you the guy who . . . of course you are. Sorry. They did something to my dad."

The man climbed the stairs, ignoring the pixie-filled air. He wasn't much to look at, though his skin was a deep, deep emerald hue. A smaller man she hadn't noticed before followed him. She hadn't noticed the smaller one because he was made of paper and very, very flat.

"Quite an infestation you have here," said the guy. "You haven't been feeding them, have you?"

"No."

Kristine grumbled to herself.

"Maybe."

The man sighed. "Chester, recon. There has to be a nest around here somewhere."

"On it, boss." The paper gnome folded into a bird and soared downstairs and away.

The guy, his name was Monster, asked to take a look at Dad, who was now wheezing and marching in place.

"How long will he keep going?" she asked.

"Until he dies," replied Monster.

"What?"

"Don't worry. I'll take care of it." He had her hold his flashlight while he flipped through a pocket-sized book and scribbled on a Post-It note.

"So it's bad to feed them?" she asked. "But they're so cute."

"So is the blue-ringed octopus, and you don't want to mess with one of those. The common house faerie is a clever little thing. It's not smart, like you or me, but it can be trained. Has a knack for household tasks, cooking cleaning, TV / VCR repair, that sort of thing. Give it a reward, and it'll be happy to do that stuff."

He slapped the Post-It onto Dad's forehead. He went stiff as a board and fell over with a thud.

"That'll keep him calm until we finish."

She knelt beside Dad and checked him. His face was a blank, but he was breathing. "He's not hurt, is he?"

"He's fine." Monster opened his satchel and rifled through the contents. "How long have you been feeding these things?"

"Couple of months, I guess. Why did they do this to my Dad? And why are they breaking stuff now?"

"When you feed one, others find out about it. Then more. Then more. Eventually, there are too many faeries and not enough work to go around. They start breaking things so that they have more stuff to fix. It makes sense to them, I suppose. The more of them around, the bolder they get. Your dad must've frightened them, so they hexed him."

Monster removed a water bottle from his bag, used his flashlight to read an incantation on the bottle's label. The liquid contents flared with a bright golden light. He squirted a bit of the liquid in the air, where it gathered into a little ball of illumination that hovered in mid-air. They walked through the house, and he lit their way with globules of magic light.

She touched one, and it popped in a flash.

"Don't do that," he said.

"Sorry."

Hundreds of pixies crawled along the walls and ceiling. They zipped through the air, chattering in their squeaky, high-pitched voices.

"Why aren't they hexing us?" she asked.

"I'm wearing my underwear inside out and backwards and my shoes on the wrong feet. Standard faerie proofing." He wiggled and twisted as he adjusted his underwear. "Wrong day to wear briefs. They probably haven't hexed you because they think you might give them something to eat."

The pixies had inflicted a lot of damage in the kitchen. The sink was busted, leaking water everywhere. The cabinets and refrigerator were opened, and all the contents spewed about haphazardly. She stepped around a pile of snack cakes and a bag of opened Cheetos.

"Why break everything when they could just take the food themselves?"

He shrugged. "Work ethic?"

The destruction didn't stop at the kitchen. They'd also done a thorough job on the living room, tearing up the sofa and smashing the television. The rug had stains on it that she deliberately avoided looking at closely.

"This is all my fault."

"Yep."

"I didn't know this would happen."

"So feeding the weird little creatures that lived in your walls seemed like a good idea?"

She said, "I don't know a lot about this magical stuff."

"All the more reason you shouldn't have been messing with it," he said. "I'm a professional, and I don't know what the hell I'm doing.

Didn't your school give you a pamphlet?"

"I lost it. I was going to ask for another one. I just never got around to it."

"Look," he said. "You seem like a bright kid. Nobody is going to watch out for you in this world. You screwed up. Be a grown up and deal with it."

Chester, the paper bird, flew into the room and folded into his gnome shape. "He's not the guy to be giving that particular speech, but he isn't wrong."

"I called you for help," said Kristine. "Not a lecture."

Monster said, "None of my business. You want to go on feeding every strange crypto you come across and getting bailed out of your messes, doesn't affect my life. Find the nest, Chester?"

"Basement, boss. It's a doozy. There must be thousands of them."

They headed toward the basement, and Monster rifled through his bag again.

"Can you get them to fix the house before they're gone?" she asked.

"Faerie repairs are always slipshod, Miss. Mostly glamour magic," said Chester. "They only work for a little while. Considering the size of the infestation, you'll be fortunate if this place doesn't come crashing down on your heads in a week once they're cleared."

"Oh."

Robots Versus Slime Monsters

A pixie landed on her hand, and the petite, beautiful little creature whistled. It looked up at Kristine with bright green eyes.

"This is all your fault."

The pixie flitted away.

Kristine noticed a hairline crack in the wall and traced it with her fingers. There was a dank stink she hadn't noticed before. The house rattled. The floor trembled under her feet like it might give way if she stepped on it too hard.

She tried pushing the blame on her parents for their divorce, Mom for not fighting for custody, Dad for buying this house. But she'd screwed up. She hadn't thought it through, and everything was all messed up now.

"My fault."

"Uh huh," said Monster as he removed a plastic container with a glowing puffball in it.

"To be fair, Miss," said Chester, "the house was likely infested before you moved in. We've had reports in this neighborhood for months now."

"Yes, you probably only made it worse faster," said Monster as he descended the stairs.

"Your boss is an asshole." She glanced around as if she'd be punished for using the word.

Chester shrugged. "Tell me about it."

Something crashed in the basement. Monster's swearing filtered up the stairs.

"Stay here, Miss. For your own safety." Chester ran down to check on Monster.

Kristine paused on the threshold, but if she couldn't fix her mistake, she could at least help someone who could.

"Mr. Monster? Chester?" She descended slowly and saw Monster at the bottom of the stairs. He'd taken a short tumble, and his legs were twisted up under his body, his arm was splayed at a weird angle.

"Holy shit."

"The little bastards set up a tripwire," said Monster. "It's worse than it looks. I'm rubbery when I'm emerald."

It wasn't much of an explanation, but she was too distracted to care.

The faeries had crumpled Chester into a ball that they playfully batted around among themselves. "This is embarrassing," he mumbled.

The basement was swarming with pixies, but none of them were flying. They covered the floor like a squirming carpet and coated the walls. A ring of shimmering mushrooms stood in the center of the basement.

"That's the nest," she said.

"Figure that out all on your own, did you?" asked Monster. He wiggled his floppy arm, and it snapped into place before going wobbly again. "Damn it."

"What do I do?" she asked.

"You should leave this to the professionals," said Monster.

Several pixies jumped on his head. They poked his eye and tugged at his hair.

"Suit yourself." Kristine turned around.

"Take the horseshoe out of my bag and drop it in the ring," he said.

She jumped over the tripwire, down the flight of stairs, and opened the bag beside his twisted body. The horseshoe caused the faeries to recoil, and their high-pitched shrieks rang in her ears.

"This isn't going to hurt them, is it?"

"It'd serve the little bastards right, but no, it won't hurt them."

She tossed the horseshoe into the circle. The mushrooms dimmed, and the pixies howled, flying in every direction, whipping past her hair and face, crawling under her clothes.

"Now open the wisp bottle!" shouted Monster above the din.

"Where is it?" she asked.

"I had it in my hands when I came downstairs! It has to be here somewhere."

Bits of the ceiling fell. An overhead pipe exploded, spraying water everywhere.

Playing a hunch, she rolled Monster to one side and found the bottle hidden under him. She twisted open the top. The pixies fell silent, and the wisp sang an ethereal melody. The faeries flew into the bottle. All of them. Within thirty seconds, they'd crammed themselves inside. The final few entranced stragglers drifted into it.

The song hypnotized her, and Kristine wanted nothing more than to stick her head in there with the rest of the pixies. Chester unfolded his crumpled body, grabbed the plastic bottle from her, and screwed the lid back on. She struggled to shake off the effects.

"Thank you."

"Just doing my job, Miss."

Monster mumbled face down in the corner.

"Sorry," said Kristine as she flipped him face up.

It took him a few minutes to straighten out. His right leg had the integrity of a wet noodle, but he could walk on it.

She studied the bottle, impossibly full of faeries. "What are you going to do with them?"

"Relocation. They'll be fine, if that's what you're asking."

Her father had stopped dancing. He was groggy after the Post-It was taken off his head, but she helped him out of the unstable house and sat him on the lawn until he recovered his senses.

"He's not going to remember this?" she asked Monster as he packed up his van.

"Not much. You won't get in trouble."

Several of the house's windows spontaneously shattered.

"That's not why I was asking."

Monster had her sign paperwork. "It's likely the place wasn't inspected properly. Or someone cut corners because they knew your dad was an incog and they could get away with it. Either way, there are agencies to help incogs cope. You can probably get a reimbursement for some of the damages." He handed her a form. "Call the number at the bottom. Don't lose this one."

She took it. "Thanks."

He drove away with his paper gnome.

Kristine joined Dad in the grass. She could smell something burning.

"I'm sorry, Kristine," he said, as if any of the blame was his.

"I'm sorry, Dad."

He gave her a curious look. "For what?"

"Just sorry. About stuff."

It didn't matter that he couldn't understand. There was always something to apologize for. All people really did was screw up and hope people would be there for them when they did. Her parents, despite it all, were always there. She took that for granted too often.

The porch collapsed.

"Who would've thought rats could do so much damage?" he said.

"Yeah. Rats." She put her arm around him and pondered a world stranger than he could ever know.

Kristine dialed emergency as fire flickered in the kitchen windows.

MY DINNER WITH ARES

Divine Misfortune

The gods are among us, and they are flawed. Divine Misfortune *was always intended to be a tribute to the myths of old, where gods were real and powerful, and where faith was a foreign concept when Zeus might show up to toss lightning bolts around in a drunken stupor. The idea of gods as human with all the advantages and disadvantages of incredible power and immortality was always appealing to me, and despite featuring some of the most powerful characters I've ever created, the story is grounded in a very mundane reality. It's* Seinfeld *meets* The Iliad, *and, even though the gods are often jerks, they have their moments of introspection. This is one of those moments.*

Ogbunabali, god of death, had many forms, most of them terrifying, but when he walked among mortals with no desire to instill dread fear in their sinful souls, he preferred the shape of a tall, angular man in a suit made of the darkest shadows and a blood red necktie. His face was a grinning black skull, and immense vulture wings sprouted from his back.

The manifestation worked by being so utterly frightening, so completely embodying the grim reality of oblivion, most mortals subconsciously chose to ignore him rather than face that truth. He walked the streets of Cleveland, ignored by nearly everyone except for one man who spotted him and fled in horror. The man must've offended the universe in some manner, and under normal circumstances, Ogbunabali would've pursued in the name of cosmic justice, but if he stopped to chase down every tainted soul he came across, he'd never get anything done.

He continued on his way, arriving at the little Greek restaurant tucked in an out of the way corner. The place could have been construed as either hole-in-the-wall or charming depending on one's inclination. It had certainly seen better days. One of the front windows had been broken and boarded up, and two young women brawled over a young man's affections on the sidewalk outside. Despite being a Greek restaurant, the Ballad of the Green Beret played from the music system.

"This must be the place," said Ogbunabali.

He moved like a shadow through the restaurant, ignored by all. He found Ares sitting at a table in the back. The god of war was hard to miss, decked out in camouflage fatigues, with a sword, shield, and Glock pistol laid on the table for everyone to see. He also wore an old-fashioned war helmet with an absurdly tall horse hair crest.

Ogbunabali sighed. Perhaps dispensing cosmic justice would be a more productive way of spending his evening. Before he could leave, Ares spotted him.

"Og, you made it!" The god of war waved him over. "Wasn't sure you were going to this time!"

Ogbunabali slipped into the opposite side of the booth. He forced a smile though with a skull for a face, it wasn't obvious. "Wouldn't miss it."

Ares pushed his weapons to one side and pounded the table. "Wench, a drink for my friend here! Wench! Wench!"

The server, a man of at least forty, came over. "Your friend, sir?"

Ogbunabali assumed a less terrifying form, that of a bottomless shadow shaped like a man. "Can I see your wine list?"

"Wine?" Ares laughed, slapped the table. "A mead, wench. And I'll take one myself. Off with you now."

The server, barely hiding his irritation, went back to the kitchen.

"Who drinks mead anymore?" asked Ogbunabali. "And I don't think wench is considered appropriate in this day and age."

"He does a wench's work. He gets called a wench."

"That's not what I meant."

Ares lifted his helmet to allow him to bite into his souvlaki, spilling bits of lamb and tomatoes on his shirt. "How have you been, Og?"

"Can't complain. And you?"

"Business is good. I'm practically drowning in tribute. These mortals do so love to slaughter one another as I'm certain a god of your particular domain is already painfully aware."

The server brought them two meads. Ogbunabali ordered the horta.

"Hardly a meal, old man."

Ares slapped the table again, and all the other customers glared in their direction. The god of war was an irritating presence, both physically and metaphysically. It was often a volatile combination. It didn't help that Ogbunabali charged the atmosphere with the specter of death. Aggravated mortals were often at their worst when reminded of their own mortality.

It was Ares's habit to pick a favorite restaurant and to visit it until his nature infected the place down to its floorboards. Depending on the location and the temperament of the locals, the place would self-destruct at its own pace. Ares would pay the owners for their loss and move on. And so it would continue.

The Ballad of the Green Beret finished and immediately restarted.

"I love this song," said Ares. "Have I told you about the time I met John Wayne?"

"Once or twice."

"Great guy. Just terrific. The Duke made war glorious, didn't he?"

"I always preferred his westerns," said Ogbunabali.

"Ah, yes." Ares leaned back and sighed. "The conquest of the Americas. What a time that was. I tell you, manifest destiny was a smashing idea. Wish I'd come up with it."

A mortal at a nearby table with a heart condition he didn't even know about clutched his chest. The condition might have gone unnoticed for decades if not for Ogbunabali's presence. The mortal's wife fanned him with concern as he drank some water.

The god of death could not stop the mortal from dying. Mortals died. It was their nature. But it needn't happen right now. Ogbunabali willed the mortal's death a few years into the future. The man's pained breathing returned to normal, and he made some silly little excuse about pushing himself too hard at the gym earlier.

His wife hugged and kissed him, and they resumed their dinner.

Ogbunabali smiled, though there was no way of knowing this in his current form. "They're so fleeting."

"What's that?" asked Ares.

"Mortal lives. They pass so quickly."

"Aren't they though? Good thing they keep breeding."

Ogbunabali took a sip of his mead. "Do you ever wonder what it would be like to be one of them?"

"No, why would I?" Ares laughed. "What's to think about? They're mortals. Not worth troubling yourself over excessively. Granted, they've accomplished a lot. With our help, of course."

"Right. Help."

"Oh, come on. Next you'll be telling me they could get along without us."

"I never said that," Ogbunabali replied. "But I do sometimes wonder."

"Preposterous. They need us."

"And we need them. What would we do without their tribute?"

"True, but they are the grass, and we are the lions."

"Lions don't eat grass."

"You know what I meant." Ares took off his helmet. "Don't tell me you're having an identity crisis, old boy?"

"No, I am a god of death. It is my nature, and I have no real desire to change it. Just an idle musing." Ogbunabali said, "Did I tell you about that business man I had to kill the other day?"

"No." Ares's disinterest was apparent. The gods were indifferent to the lives and deaths of ordinary mortals, and gods of war were especially so.

Ogbunabali told the tale regardless.

"He was a follower of mine. We had an arrangement, you see. I kept his death at bay, and he repaid me with tributes of animal sacrifices and burnt offerings. It worked out nicely for a few hundred years, but I can only do so much. Death comes for all men, and not even I can change that. But seeing as how he was such a dedicated sort who never missed a payment, I felt I should deliver the bad news personally."

"Yes, very thoughtful of you," said Ares.

Ogbunabali continued, aware that Ares was only half listening. The god of death was talking mostly to himself anyway.

"I visited him at his home. He wasn't happy to see me. They never are. I can't blame them for that, I suppose." He sighed. "He didn't take it well. He had more years than most mortals, but in the end, he said it wasn't enough. He needed more. Understand this was a man who had accomplished great things. He had wealth, power, family. And he was also a genuinely nice guy. Not perfect by any means, but he had made this world a better place in his time than how he'd found it. Something I pointed out to him in hopes of helping with the transition."

"Very sensible," mumbled Ares.

"It didn't matter. He offered me everything he had. He offered to burn every dollar of his fortune for just a little more time. He'd erect statues in my honor. He'd have a movie made glorifying me. He had Steven Spielberg on his speed dial. Said I'd have first choice of casting and final script approval."

Ares perked up. "Sidney Poitier. That's who I would say should play you."

Ogbunabali ignored the remark. "I told him it was a very generous offer, but I'm not that kind of god. I work in the shadows. And mortals have no interest in the exploits of a death god in any case."

"True. Remember Tuoni's film?"

"Don't remind me. What a dreadful self-indulgence."

Ogbunabali's food arrived. He picked at the plate with little interest.

"I explained that it just didn't work that way, and that, while I could keep him going a while longer, it was at the point that my favor output was exceeding his tribute. All very logical from a business perspective, and that he, a very successful businessman, should have understood. He didn't."

"I could've told you that," said Ares. "Mortals only truly value their lives when they're about to lose them. It's good for my business at least. If they paused to think before throwing themselves once more into the breach, there wouldn't be much for me to do."

Ogbunabali said, "I almost let him live."

"What?" Ares slapped the table hard enough to knock over his mug. The mead spilled across the tablecloth, leaving a red stain in the image of a skull, no doubt influenced by the presence of the gods.

"I said almost," said Ogbunabali.

Ares snorted. "Not a very death god thing to do. One mortal life means nothing, Og. You should know that by now."

"Actually, I'm pretty sure one mortal life is all that matters. At least to the mortal that lives it."

The god of war laughed, and his amusement caused a fistfight to break out in the neighboring booth.

"We all get sentimental now and then, Og, but that's no reason to—"

"I could've afforded it. I've got enough surplus favor from my other investments."

"It's not a question of spare favor," said Ares. "The whole system works as a free exchange of tribute and favor. If someone starts getting more favor than they've earned it sets a bad precedent. I could see if this mortal was a great warrior or hero—"

"He was just a guy," said Ogbunabali. "Successful and influential, but not a legend in the making."

"If he doesn't serve your greater glory or bring you bragging rights, why would you even consider it?"

"He seemed like a nice guy. This world can always use more nice guys."

Ares shrugged. "I don't get it."

Ogbunabali found this unsurprising. Ares had always been a dim-witted sort.

"Do you ever wonder what it would be like?" asked Ogbunabali. "To be a god of life and joy, to have mortals welcome your arrival?"

"I don't have to wonder. The Spartans loved me. Temples and statues everywhere. Sacrifices and offerings galore. Those were the days."

Smiling, Ares gazed wistfully into the distance.

"Nobody likes me," said Ogbunabali. "No one has ever liked me. They tolerate me. They bargain with me. They fear me. But no one has ever been happy to see me."

"I don't know what you're complaining about. At least as a god of death, you have job security. In ten thousand years, if things keep going as they're going, the mortals might get over their obsession with killing each other. Unlikely, yes, but not impossible. Won't be much tribute for myself at that point. I'll be no better off than that one fellow? You know the one I'm thinking of. God of the strigil. Oh, what is his name, again? Doesn't matter, I suppose. That was a god who thought he had everything figured out. Then along comes soap, and now where is he?

"Not you though. You, Og, will always have a place among mortals as long as they are mortal. That's nothing to sneeze at, and you have to admit that you're good at it."

"I'm the best," admitted Ogbunabali. "But—"

"But nothing. You're Ogbunabali, god of death, slayer of transgressors."

"Yeah, about that. I kind of . . . let one go, recently."

Ares slammed the table again, but Ogbunabali caught his mug before it could spill.

"You don't let them go. This isn't catch and release."

"You haven't heard the story."

"Fine. Tell it to me. But let me get another drink first."

Ares ordered three tequila shots and downed them one after the other before allowing Ogbunabali to continue.

"It was a couple of weeks ago," said the death god. "I was on referral. Picked up some contract work from Fury Central. They're always short staffed. I get this order that this young mortal, twenty-five years old, has transgressed and now needs to be punished. Nothing new. I've done it thousands of times, track down some poor idiot who dared break some sacred law, kill him as an example. Standard procedure.

"Usually, they don't tell me why, and I don't ask. Nature of contract work. But this time, I don't dispatch the mortal as soon as I find him. I stick around and watch him for a while. I don't know why. Call it morbid curiosity."

"Bad move," said Ares. "You can't get too close to these mortals. I've seen enough promising young warriors die ignobly on the battlefield to know that."

He frowned as the faces of countless nameless mortals flashed through his memory. He remembered them all, even if he didn't think of them often. Even a god of war could find the recollection frightening in its sheer volume. He countered the memory by distracting himself by humming along with The March of the Gladiators blaring out of the sound system speakers. The tune wasn't nearly as terrifying since the circus had taken it for its own, but it still warmed Ares's blood.

Ogbunabali sat quietly while Ares struggled to focus again.

"Ah, yes." Ares cleared his throat. "Got a bit distracted there. You were saying something about following this marked mortal around. Please, continue."

"So I'm following him, and I know there's something wrong because he has the stain of offense upon him. But it's not right. There's something off about it. It was like he was marked, but he wasn't acting like it. Transgressors almost always manifest some sign of guilt, some gnawing subconscious pressure that they've done something horrible. They might wash their hands excessively or become hermits or quickly become exhausted from sleep plagued with nightmares.

"It's not universal. Some mortals are just so amoral that they just don't feel anything about it, but those types don't usually end up on my radar. And when I run into them . . ." --Ogbunabali shivered.-- " . . .

there are mortals even gods should fear.

"But while I sense regrets in this kid, and while he isn't without sins, I don't end up sensing any cosmic-level wrongdoing on his part.

"It's difficult to explain, but it comes down to this mortal is just not giving off the right vibes. So I call Fury Central, and I ask what his crime is. They don't want to tell me at first, but I keep pressing until I get a supervisor who passes me to another supervisor who passes me to another until I finally find someone who knows and who is willing to tell me. Turned out the mortal was in a car accident. Ended up putting the guy in the other car in the hospital. But here's the catch. The other guy in this incident just happens to be a demigod, and while his injuries aren't life threatening, his divine parent takes offense and has enough pull with Fury Central to contract a hit."

"Well, if he dared hit a demigod, it seems an open and shut case," said Ares. "I can see feeling bad for the poor sod, but he wouldn't be the first mortal to earn the wrath of the heavens by simply making a wrong turn."

"That's what I thought first, but it still isn't sitting right. So I do some research, check the accident reports, interview a few witnesses."

"A bit out of step with your usual obligations, isn't it, Og?"

"I know, but I couldn't stop myself. I look into it, all the while making excuses to Fury Central that I'm only waiting for the right time to strike. For maximum ironic effect, I tell them. And the more I find out, the less I like. The demigod in question was driving drunk. Ran a red light. And while he got the worst of it, my mark didn't come out unscathed. He ended up breaking his leg in a couple of places, and he's stuck with a limp, even after recovery. Meanwhile, the demigod gets a miraculous recovery, via mom or dad's connections, and is barely inconvenienced by it in the end. Everyone agreed that the mark wasn't at fault, and that it was a miracle in itself that he wasn't killed."

"Hardly a miracle," said Ares. "Just a bit of luck."

Ogbunabali laughed. "Exactly. All things considered, he's lucky enough to not die, and now, I'm supposed to kill him."

"I find it hard to believe you haven't killed mostly innocent mortals before."

"I have. Not every mark is guilty of slaughtering their children and serving them in a stew. The man who killed the last Mauritian flying fox had committed no great sin, but it was still my job to see him punished for the offense, so I did.

"But this case was just too petty. Worse, it was wrong. I didn't end up laying a finger on him."

"But won't they send someone else?"

"Do you think they're that organized? I call in and report justice has been delivered, the kid's name is crossed off their score sheet, tossed in a dead file somewhere. End of story."

"Surely, there must be some manner of confirmation process."

"Volume is high. The odds are slim that anyone will do any checking. I'm keeping an eye on the situation, just in case."

"So you've appointed yourself this young mortal's protector then? What tribute does he offer you in return that can be worth the risk?"

"None. He doesn't even know I'm around, and I intend to keep it that way."

Ares scratched the stubble on his chin. "Sounds a bit odd to me, Og."

"I am a god of death, and I don't imagine many mortals would take much comfort having me watching over them, and if I told him, I'd have to explain everything. That wouldn't be very comforting either. It's better this way."

"It's your call," said Ares, "but I can't say I understand what you get out of it."

"I don't really get anything out of it," replied Ogbunabali. "That's what makes it worth doing. You should try it sometime, Ares. If only for a chance to see new horizons."

Ares chuckled. "I think not. I prefer my horizons exactly where they are."

The gods enjoyed the rest of their meal without discussing anything more troubling than the weather. Afterward, they settled the check and made plans to meet up sometime next decade. The god of death transformed into a flock of bats and flew from the restaurant and into the night.

Ares, nursing a scotch and soda, sat in the booth. When closing time came around, he walked aimlessly through the city streets, lost in his thoughts, until happening upon a fender bender that drew his attention.

What would've been a simple act of exchanging insurance information became more violent as one of the drivers, a hulking brute already teeming with aggression, responded poorly to Ares's presence. The brute grabbed the shorter, meeker man by the collar and shouted at him.

The god of war didn't normally notice these events, any more than the gods of rain might notice the clouds that trailed alongside them. But this time, Ares did notice, and he would've happily watched the stronger man smack the weaker fellow around, as was the rightful way of this world as far as the god of war was concerned. He decided to switch things up for once.

Ares filled the meek mortal with the tiniest portion of righteous strength, and with one mighty strike, the brute was laid low. The winner stared at his hands, amazed at what forces had seized him, even more amazed at what he'd managed to do. Then, to Ares's surprise, the mortal helped the larger man up and apologized. What would've surely cooled Ares's blood with disgust, he now found intriguing. There was none of the conqueror spirit in this weak mortal, and he was hardly worthy of what Ares had to offer.

And yet . . .

Perhaps, mused Ares, he had limited himself by sticking with only the more belligerent of these creatures. Perhaps there was something to be said for helping the little guy for no other reason than to see how it might play out.

The drivers exchanged information, and got back into their cars. The meek mortal noticed Ares watching him. Ares waved, and the mortal waved back.

Ares put on his helmet and pondered eternity. Even for a god, it was a long time, and there might be something to be said for expanding one's horizons, after all.

"I'll be seeing you around, friend," he said to the Hyundai's driver.

The god of war transformed into a red stag and bound away into the sky.

PIZZA MADNESS

Chasing the Moon

My original ode to H.P. Lovecraft was a tough nut to crack, if I can be honest. Chasing the Moon drove me a little bit crazy. In the end, I was very happy with the way it turned out, and when I think about it now, if it hadn't been so difficult, I'm not sure it would've been the cosmic horror story it ultimately became. This short story, an homage to Poe with Lovecraftian influences, was easier. Maybe I sacrificed enough of my sanity to the original novel to make it so.

My ending began at Pizza Madness.

"I'm here about the delivery driver job," I said.

"Do you have a car?" asked Mr. Han.

I nodded.

He dropped a stack of pizzas before me, along with a slip of order forms. "Deliver these."

This was how my doom started. There was no warning, no crack of thunder. There were only pizzas to deliver and minimum wage plus tips. So it went that I delivered those pizzas and collected my earnings. I would go home, and my girlfriend would complain about the stench of grease and cheese. I would shower to appease her. It worked, but after a few weeks, I could still smell it. It oozed from my pores, and even if no one else acted like they could detect the odor, I knew they could. Even if they couldn't.

My girlfriend, I can't remember her name anymore (though I think it started with an A) sat farther on the couch from me. She laughed less. She couldn't wait to jump in the shower after sex. After a while, I could smell the pizza on her.

How terribly it reeked. How awful that horrid perfume of peperoni and kalamata olives.

"You should get a new job," she'd said once.

I nodded as if I agreed, but what she couldn't understand was that I'd been marked by the pizza in a way that could never be undone. I'd spent too many hours serving the pizza to ever escape it. I wasn't a delivery driver. I was its chauffeur. People didn't call for me. They called for the pizza, and when I brought it, they were never eager to see me. It was the pizza they desired, and I was merely a beast of burden to be smiled at, to be given a few extra bucks for my service. Even this was only to ensure that I had a car and enough gas to keep doing this.

Pizza Madness held me in its clutches. Escape was impossible.

Robots Versus Slime Monsters

My girlfriend broke up with me sometime after that. Time became meaningless to me. There were only the days when I delivered pizzas and the days when I didn't, when I sat in my apartment, stared blankly at a television, and thought about the deliveries I would have to make soon.

I think harsh words were exchanged in the breakup. I think she said ugly things in an effort to stir my passions, and I would have loved her for that if I could've. As we shared one last hug, I smelled the dough in her hair and the sausage wafting from her neck, and I realized if she didn't leave now, the pizza would claim her forever too. So I did my last sensible act and released her, hoping it wasn't too late. As she walked into the night, crying, I thought I should feel something. But my soul was clogged with cheese and marinara sauce, and if there had been something between us, it was buried so deep that I'd never find it again.

Once she was gone, I had more time to devote to the pizza, and I was happy for a while. Pizza Madness needed me in a way that no one else could. Pizza Madness would always be there for me so long as I had a car and knew my way around the city. I drove its streets with unhindered purpose, and sometimes, through the windshield, I would see strange creatures and a sky alive with a thousand, thousand pitiless eyes staring down at the city.

None of them saw me. I was too small to be seen. I was an insignificant thing, but I had the pizza. It was enough. It had to be. It was all I could ever have.

I started picking up more shifts. Mr. Han was happy to give them to me. He didn't ask why. Mr. Han served the pizza too. He knew why.

My last dinner with my family was a holiday of some sort. I can't remember which, though I think it started with a T.

I think they asked about my life. I mumbled my replies, and all the while, I thought about how empty their expressions of concerns were. They didn't care. They'd never cared. My sister (her name started with an R, I believe) gave me one last hug. It was a tentative frightened embrace, no doubt repelled by the aura of cheese I carried with me at all times.

"Don't be a stranger," she said.

"Uh huh."

I don't think I ever saw her again after that. Although once, while on a delivery, someone who looked like her tried talking to me. I simply ignored her.

People stopped calling me for which I was grateful.

I was content. Not happy. Happiness was a lie reserved for other people, but as long as I had the pizza (or more honestly, as long as it had me), I could live, knowing my purpose in a way that few men did.

Then I saw him.

The Old Man.

I'd never seen another delivery boy at Pizza Madness. I assumed Mr. Han had others for those days I didn't work, but now, I always worked. There was no need for another. I had dedicated my life to serve, and I asked for nothing in return save the knowledge that the pizza needed me.

But on that day, I realized that this was untrue. I could always be replaced. I was nothing. I was a mote of dust riding the city streets with no purpose, no reason for being. This was made clear by the Old Man. He walked out of Pizza Madness carrying a box, and a consuming weakness staggered me. He might have been a customer, but Pizza Madness never had walk-ins. He wore the official red and yellow jacket that I wore. By the time I recovered my senses, he had climbed into his own car and driven away.

I confronted Mr. Han. "Who was that?"

"Delivery boy," he said.

"I'm the delivery boy," I replied.

Mr. Han, his hands kneading dough, shrugged. "He's the special delivery boy. He handles special deliveries."

"I can handle special deliveries," I said.

He shook his head. "You don't want that job."

He was right. I didn't want it.

But I needed it.

Mr. Han dropped my latest stack of sacred deliveries on the counter. "Get to work."

I performed my duty as always, and I was convinced if I showed Mr. Han my true devotion, he would get rid of the Old Man (I think his name started with a B or C) and give me all the deliveries.

He didn't.

Every day, I'd ask. Every day, he'd shake his head.

"You don't want that job."

More and more, I'd see the Old Man. We'd pass each other on our duties, but we were never in the shop at the same time. Always he carried one pizza. Always, he would mock me. My pizzas were ordinary things, but he had the special deliveries. Wasn't I worthy? Hadn't I given everything I had? What more could it ask of me?

I knew the answer, but it was only while eating my nightly dinner of pepperoni and cheese that I accepted it.

So one day, I shirked my sacred duty. I walked out with a handful of pizzas that sat in my passenger seat, getting cold. They whispered their dark desires to me, but I ignored them as I waited.

Waited for the Old Man.

How long I waited, I couldn't say. My deliveries grew angrier with each passing moment, but the rage of the bubbling cheeses faded as it cooled. It was empowering to realize that while the pizza was greater than I could ever be, I still had some power over it.

The Old Man appeared eventually. The shop had closed, but I knew this was only a trick. I waited, and as I grew hungrier, I contemplated eating one of my deliveries. It was a terrible thought, an abandonment of everything I believed. I didn't do more than think about it, but even then, I wondered if my sins had already damned me, despite my months (years? decades?) of service.

The darkened door to the shop opened, and the Old Man stepped out, carrying his special delivery. He drove away, and he must have surely seen me following him. But the delivery was everything, and I respected his dedication, pale as it was next to my own.

He came to a stop in front of an old apartment building, and while he crossed the street, I plowed into him. He only stood there as my headlights bore down on him, and though I saw his face for only a moment, I thought he was smiling before he bounced off my hood, smashing his head into the windshield glass. His body rolled to a stop.

I hadn't thought about witnesses, but there were none. The street was empty, as unlikely as it might seem, and as I scrambled to check on him, I was sure to grab my tire iron. The Old Man lay in a broken, twisted heap. Somehow, he'd managed to keep hold of his delivery. I grabbed the battered box, but he refused to release it.

"Let go!" I screamed. "Let go!"

He looked up into my eyes. His face was covered in blood and bruises. He spoke, barely understandable with his broken jaw and blood-filled throat.

"You don't want it."

I could see that he was every bit as dedicated to this task as I was, but in the end, I couldn't allow him to live. I offered him as my sacrifice to the pizza, the second greatest offering I could grant. I can't remember doing it. I can only remember the red-soaked tire iron, and how, even dead, he refused to release the box until I broke his fingers. His dying grip was pressed into the cardboard.

I realized a thousand witnesses had seen my act. They stared down from the sky, and for the first time, they saw me. For the first time, I was important enough to be seen. I cackled with delight, clutching the box to my chest, jumping into my car and driving home without delay. The special delivery wanted to be opened, but I waited until we were safe in my apartment before doing so. Anything else would've been profane.

There was an eviction notice on the door, and the manager (his name started with an S, I think) had changed the locks. I used my bloody tire iron to get inside, and in the darkened room, chuckling to myself, I opened the special delivery.

Empty.

Enraged, I hurled the box away, but my fury dissolved almost as soon as it came. I didn't know what I'd expected. I'd lost everything in my servitude, and my act hadn't been one of obedience or devotion, but of hubris and sacrilege. I'd betrayed the pizza, and it had repaid me in kind.

I sat in the dark, laughing, crying. I'd damned myself, and the painful truth was that I would do so again, given the opportunity.

The box shuffled across the floor. I wiped my tears away to watch as it dragged itself by a single long tendril. The box, the thing, the box and the thing for they were one and the same, hopped around in comical bursts. More writhing tentacles and a single giant eye on a long stalk pushed out of the box. The thing grew bigger as it stumbled blindly. Its eye was mostly closed, save for a small slit.

The room grew darker with each passing moment.

Someone knocked on my door. I could only stare at the thing as it prepared to destroy me for my transgressions. A tentacle wrapped around my ankle, and some small instinct caused me to lash out with my tire iron. A second undulating limb ripped the weapon from my hand and threw it across the room. The thing squirmed its way up my legs. Its eye opened a little more, to peer into my putrid, imperfect soul.

A. Lee Martinez

The door exploded in a blast of lightning. Both myself and the thing paused as another tentacle creature with one eye floated into the room. Behind it followed a fuzzy green thing with a head that was only a mouth and another larger mouth set in its round belly.

"Ah hell, we might be too late," said the floating eyeball.

His eye crackled with strange energies. A moment later, a bolt of cosmic power blew a hole through the wall. And the wall behind that. And the wall behind that. The pizza thing shrieked as its blackened, slimy flesh sizzled.

"I got this," said the furry green beast as he seized one of the pizza god's tentacles and shoved it into his gut.

"Don't eat the guy," said the floating eye.

The eating monster grumbled with his mouths full as he chewed down the pizza god. It was an ordeal. My god didn't want to be devoured, and he fought against every bite. But the green creature slowly consumed his prey, and I could only sit there and watch.

The green monster wiped his chin. His cheeks bulged as he spit up a little bit of tentacle before swallowing it down again.

"Are you going to be able to keep that down?" asked the eyeball.

"Are you kidding me?" He chewed and gulped. "This is what I do. I could probably use an antacid though. Lesser horrors always give me gas."

He belched.

"What have you done?" I asked. "That was my god."

"That was my pizza," said the green monster. "And you're crazy if you think I'm going to pay for it. Forget about the tip, for that matter."

"That was yours?" I asked.

"Special delivery," said the eyeball. "A thing from another world that doesn't belong in this universe. Not that we do either, but at least we try to limit the damage."

I tried standing on shaky legs but could only fall to my knees before these terrible creatures. "Are you going to kill me now?"

"We'd be doing you a favor if we did," said the green monster. "And I am a bit peckish."

"Hold your appetite, big guy," said the eyeball. "Greater good. He has to live."

Laughter wracked my body. I wasn't living. I hadn't been living for a very long time.

"Yeah, but it still seems like a rotten proposition for the poor guy," said the eating monster.

"It's a cruel universe," said the eyeball, and there was some sympathy in his voice.

They left me there, in my darkened hollow. How long I lay there, sobbing or laughing, I couldn't say. But eventually, I climbed out of the emptiness and, with nothing else to do, I went back to Pizza Madness.

Mr. Han was there. I wanted to tell him of my crimes against the Old Man, against the pizza. Before I could, he dropped a box on the counter.

"Special delivery," he said.

I took the box without thinking, and realized that by slaying the Old Man, I had proved myself worthy after all. I smiled. It'd all been worth it. I'd been forgiven my sins, and the prize was mine.

"Hey, kid," said Mr. Han. "Remember. I said you didn't want this job."

He was wrong. I wanted it more than anything, and as I climbed into my car, I realized I knew exactly where to go for this delivery. I would always know.

I pulled to a stop outside the old apartment building. The same building I'd killed the Old Man outside of. I knocked on the front door, and the green monster answered.

"Right on time." He took the pizza from me and shoved it into his mouth, swallowing it whole. The thing inside the box shrieked a little and the green monster had to shove a bit of tentacle down. He handed me a twenty dollar bill and with both his mouths smiling, he instructed me to "Keep the change."

I returned to Pizza Madness, but there were no more special deliveries today. Perhaps tomorrow. Perhaps the day after that. I would carry the thing in the box to the green monster, whom would eat it for another day.

I am the keeper of the wretched thing. The eternal warden of that which cannot die but must never be let loose. It lives forever, in the box that I carry and feed to the grinning green hungry god. Though I cannot live forever myself, I know that one day, when I am the Old Man, I shall see headlights bearing down on me in the darkness, ending my duty, beginning it anew in the unkind illusion of time.

CINDY AND CRAGG

Emperor Mollusk versus the Sinister Brain

When first creating the Saturnites, a race of rock-based aliens, as antagonists to evil genius, Emperor Mollusk, I knew I had to do more with them. Cragg has a blink and you'll miss it part in the original novel, but like Ogbunabali, god of death, Cragg won me over instantly. This was a guy, down on his luck, living on a world he didn't really belong on, disgraced and thoroughly defeated. He's down and most definitely out, but life goes on. I think we can all relate.

Cindy hated dates.

She hated first dates even more.

Thankfully, this wasn't a date. It was just a social gathering of employees in a Mexican restaurant. She didn't even want to go, but it was a corporate morale booster thing. If she didn't go, she'd have to make excuses to all the other employees and have to talk to a manager (maybe two) about her lack of teamwork. She would have to resist the urge the entire time to point out that she was a cashier at a supermarket and that the job hardly required commando-level training or loyalty.

So she'd go. It would be easier to give up one evening of her life rather than deal with all that.

"Mom, you aren't going to wear that, are you?"

Laura stood in the doorway. She was at that age when she knew better than her mother and wasn't shy about saying so. Not that she was a rude child. Just a little more self-assured on certain subjects than she had any right to be. It was the blessing of youth, and Cindy was reluctant to crush it. The world would get around to that soon enough.

"What's wrong with it?" asked Cindy. The blue dress wasn't anything fancy, but it looked nice. She was self-conscious of her butt. The years had added a few pounds, and she didn't take care of herself like she should. Although she noted with complete self-awareness that taking care of oneself usually translated into denying the slow, inevitable advance of years.

"What's wrong with it?" she asked again.

Laura shrugged. She loved to shrug. Sometimes, with one shoulder. Sometimes, with both. Sometimes, silently. Sometimes, with an exasperated sigh. But it always meant the same thing. Mom didn't get it.

Cindy freely admitted this was probably true.

"So who is this guy?" asked Laura.

"Just a guy I work with." Cindy was vague in hopes Laura would lose interest in the question. It failed. Ironically, if Cindy had tried talking to her about it, she probably would've.

"Ah, yes, Craig the cashier from the supermarket," said Laura. "Aim high, Mom."

"He's a stock boy," mumbled Cindy. "And his name's Cragg."

"Whatever."

She liked saying whatever a lot too. And if she was in the mood, she might even combine it with a shrug, though that was usually more effort than she was willing to employ.

"I think it's good that you're going out," said Laura. "Been—what-- like two years since the last one?"

Cindy closed her eyes and put her hands to her face. "God, please, don't remind me."

Laura put her hand on Cindy's shoulder. "Mom, you're cool. The dress is cool. You'll be fine. And I'm sure Cragg is . . . well . . . I doubt he's cool considering he's a stock boy, but I'm sure he's cool enough. You don't want him to be too cool, right?"

She smiled and gave Cindy a hug. It was times like these, buried under the shrugs and whatevers, that Cindy decided she had a pretty good daughter.

The doorbell rang.

"I'll get it."

Laura sprang from the room and toward the front door before Cindy could stop her. Cindy groaned. She'd hoped Laura would be out with her friends tonight, but she'd known this was coming.

"Holy crap!" shouted Laura from the front door.

Cindy took a second to comb her hair once more and adjust her dress. She considered changing out heels and into flats. This wasn't supposed to be a high heels kind of thing. But the heels were already on, and she just wanted to get this over with.

Cragg, a hulking mass of stone in a bright blue tuxedo with fringe around the collar, stood in the center of the living room with some red roses in his hand.

"Mom, why didn't you mention your date was a Saturnite?"

Cindy prided herself as a good mother, though she was tempted to slap the smirk off her daughter's face.

"I didn't think it was important."

Cragg awkwardly thrust the bouquet at Cindy. "These for you."

She didn't take them, and he frowned at the flowers.

"Lopez in meats said this was Terran tradition."

Laura took the bouquet and transferred it to her mother. "They're lovely. Aren't they, Mom?" She elbowed Cindy, who nodded.

"Yes, yes, lovely."

"So what are you two crazy kids up to tonight?" asked Laura.

"A bonding exercise with the rest of the Super Plus Mart squadron," said Cragg.

"Sounds good," said Laura. She nudged Cindy again.

"Yes, sounds good."

This was a bad idea. She sized up the giant alien of stone. What the hell had she been thinking with this?

"So Cragg, I bet you killed a lot of Terrans during the Saturnite wars," said Laura.

Cindy wished her daughter would stop saying things. Although she was the only one keeping the awkward silence at bay.

Cragg nodded. "Yes. Many."

"Too bad about what happened to Saturn in the end though," said Laura. "No hard feelings."

He frowned.

Cindy glanced at her watch in an exaggerated manner, like a pantomime clown acting it out. "Look at the time. We need to get going."

She hustled Cragg out the front door. A big rig truck was parked in front of their house. Like all Saturnites, Cragg was every bit as heavy as a being of living stone would be, and he needed a vehicle with muscle to get him around.

"Have fun, you two," said Laura. "Don't do anything I wouldn't do. Have her home by eleven, big guy."

Cragg helped Cindy into the truck with a gentle palm push on her butt, then climbed in on his side. The rig rocked as he did so.

"Sorry about that," she said. "She thinks she's clever."

"You let your offspring determine your curfew?"

"It was a joke. She was joking."

He grunted.

God, she hated first dates.

***

They didn't talk in the truck. Cindy thought about saying something, but she wasn't sure what to say. Then she settled on "Nice night, isn't it?", but Cragg opened his mouth as if to speak just then and it threw her off.

He was only yawning.

Cragg didn't appear to mind the silence, but he was hard to read. Not that he talked a lot. He was a pretty quiet guy. Saturnites were quiet generally. She didn't know a whole heck of a lot about their culture, but she had yet to meet one who liked small talk.

The longer the silence lasted, the more impenetrable it became. It was only when they reached the restaurant and climbed out of the truck that she felt enabled to break it.

"Why did you ask me out?"

He blinked at her. Blankly.

"Why did you say yes?"

"You can't answer a question with a question."

Cragg didn't reply.

"If you aren't going to tell me, we can call this thing off right now," she said. "Probably better if we did."

"You remind me of my favored vulkon in my original birthing basalt."

"Vulkon?"

"There isn't an exact Terran translation. It is a sort of caretaker who supervises new young."

"Like a mother?"

Cragg nodded. "Something like that, yes."

"So I remind you of your mother?"

"Yes. In a way."

He smiled, though his smiles were slight and his gray rock face devoid of many features. It took him a while to notice she wasn't smiling back at him.

"Is that offensive?"

She said, "No. Not really. It's not something a girl likes to hear, but at least it's honest."

"Why did you say yes?" he asked.

"I'm a forty-something divorcee with a kid and a dead end job. It's not as if I've got a lot of prospects. But just for the record, I don't think we should call this a date. If the others ask, we aren't together. We're just arriving . . . together."

"Agreed."

He walked away without offering her his arm, and she hobbled after him. It was a struggle to keep up. She should've worn flats.

She studied him from behind. He wasn't conventionally handsome, but he was large and powerful, and he embodied a stolid stoicism that she found attractive in Terran males. He might have been made out of stone (She still wasn't clear if Saturnites were actually made of stone or just resembled it) but he seemed to possess all the reliability and stability of the mountains. Or perhaps that was simply her imagination.

They found their coworkers sitting around a table in a small private room in the back of the restaurant. Despite reservations, she entered the room beside Cragg. All eyes turned toward them, and conversation died down. The mariachi music playing over the sound system made things somehow more awkward.

Cindy waved. "Hello."

Everyone returned to their conversations, and Anthony, the grocery store manager, came over to greet them. He wore a big smile and a blue sports jacket.

"Hey, you two. Glad you could make it." He glanced between them. "You two aren't here—"

"This isn't a date," said Cragg.

Cindy scooted a few inches away from him. "We just came together."

Anthony winked. His wink was perverse. His thin mustache and smarmy demeanor helped. Upon first meeting him, Cindy had told herself it was unfair to judge a man for such choices and that just because she disliked jewelry on men (and wasn't too fond of it on women either), she needn't think the worst of him because he wore a pinkie ring. It was only after she'd gotten to know him that she gave herself permission to hold a low opinion of Anthony.

"You're looking good, babe," he said.

"She doesn't like to be called babe," said Cragg.

"Oh, it's a party, big guy. Lighten up." Anthony smacked Cragg on the arm. "We're just here to have a good time. Isn't that right, babe?"

"Right," she said.

"Mind if I borrow the little lady for a bit?"

"Actually—" said Cragg.

"Great. Thanks." Anthony put his hand on her back, a little lower than she was comfortable with, and pushed her away. Anthony directed her to a corner of the room. "Really? You'd rather come with Mount Everest over there than me?"

"We didn't come together," she replied. "We just came . . . together."

"Hey, I get it. You're into weird stuff. It's cool." He grinned. "Maybe we could be into weird stuff together."

Cragg loomed over Anthony. "Is there a problem here, Cindy?"

"No problem." She shoved Anthony aside. "Let's grab a drink."

"Would you like me to crush him for you?" asked Cragg in a low whisper.

"Oh, don't trouble yourself."

"No trouble. I've always hated that guy." He chuckled.

She didn't know if he meant it or if he was being nice. Either way, it was sweet of him to offer.

No one else commented on Cragg and Cindy's indeterminate dating state, and things were going smoothly enough until Cindy once again found herself cornered. Not by Anthony, this time, but by a tall Saturnite server with a polished obsidian face. The Saturnite was taller than Cragg, but thinner. Positively svelte by Saturnite standards, though still wide and stocky.

Cindy waved away the server's tray of quesadilla bites. "No, thank you. I'm good."

She tried to maneuver around the server, but the Saturnite stepped in her way.

"What do you think you're doing, Terran?"

"Excuse me?"

"You aren't worthy of him."

"Who?"

The server rumbled her displeasure like a miniature earthquake rolling out of her throat. "Wasn't our defeat and the near destruction of our world enough for your people? Dare you humiliate our greatest warriors by taking them on as your concubines?"

"Okay, first of all, you invaded Terra. We were just defending ourselves. Secondly, he asked me out. Thirdly, this is not a date."

Cragg came over, and the Saturnite server quickly lumbered away.

"Was Ignis bothering you?" replied Cragg.

"Do you know her?"

He nodded.

"Wow. Small world, huh?"

The Saturnite server glared at them with her topaz eyes.

"What's her problem?" asked Cindy.

"Ignis has always had a temper, and she was extremely territorial. It was why we broke up, I suppose."

"Wait a minute. You used to date?"

"For about a year."

"Oh, that's not . . . wait. Are we talking Terran years or Saturn years?"

"Saturn," he mumbled.

"Great. That's like thirty Terran years, right?"

"Twenty-nine point seven," he said.

"Oh hell. I need a drink."

She went to the bar and cut in front of the line. A few people grumbled, but she felt it was justified. She found a seat by herself and sipped her Jack and Coke. Cragg gave her some space, and Anthony circled like a hungry vulture waiting for the right moment to strike. Ignis disappeared into the kitchen and didn't return.

When she was finished, Cindy quietly sneaked out of the party and sat on the curb outside the restaurant. She stared at her cell phone, considering whether to call a taxi or not. It'd be better to just hit the abort button and call it a night. She could explain everything to Cragg next time she saw him. He'd understand. It wasn't like this was a date.

"Hey, babe, what'cha doing out here, all alone?" asked Anthony from behind her, his smarm dialed up to twelve.

"Not now," she said. "I'm not in the mood."

"Babe, I'm hurt." He sat beside her. "Y'know, I've always liked you. I've always had this thing for meatier women."

"Holy hell, Anthony," she said before she could stop herself. "Are you a moron or something?"

He looked absolutely puzzled. "What? It's a compliment."

"I'm going to give you some advice," she said. "Don't take it as any kind of encouragement to keep hitting on me because—and I want to be absolutely clear about this—you and me, it just isn't happening. Ever. Never ever."

"Babe—"

"Don't call me Babe. I hate that. And when a woman tells you she hates something, don't do it. Hell, if a guy tells you he hates something, don't do it. It's just basic common courtesy. It's how most Terrans make an effort to relate to each other."

He opened his mouth to speak, but she kept going.

"And for heaven's sake, don't call a woman meaty. Just don't do it. Even if it's meant as a compliment. It's stupid. And I'm not meaty. I'm just not a size zero, and I'd appreciate it if you stopped trying to make me feel guilty about that.

"But the most important thing I'm going to tell you is this. I am not a conquest. I'm a person, and I don't need to be conquered. When I tell you to buzz off, I'm not playing coy. It's not meant as encouragement. We are not playing a game of seduction here. You are an idiot, and I've dated enough idiots in my life to know better by now."

Anthony frowned. She doubted he could absorb much of what she was telling him, but if even a sliver got past his obtuse defenses and made things easier on the next woman he set his sights on, she'd consider it a major victory.

There might be reprisals. He was her superior. She'd deal with them if she had to.

"Oh, and either learn to grow a real mustache or shave that thing off," she said.

He walked away without saying another word, and Cindy put her phone away. "You can come out now."

Cragg stepped out of the shadows where he'd been hiding. "How long have you known I was here?"

"A while. You're not exactly the stealthy type. Why didn't you say anything?"

"It is disrespectful to interfere in another warrior's battles," he said. "You handled yourself ably."

She smiled. "Ah, thanks."

"I can still crush him for you if you would like."

"I'll keep that in mind. Would you mind if we called it an early evening? This thing has been a beating."

"If that's what you want."

The Saturnite's face was difficult to read, but Cindy was getting the hang of it. Enough to see hints of disappointment. "Oh, it's not you, Cragg. If it was just you and me, I think it could've been fun."

"Perhaps we could do something else sometime then?" he asked

"Yeah. Maybe." She hated that she didn't have the guts to just tell him no. She was fairly certain he'd accept the answer, but she wasn't in the mood for the conversation if he didn't.

The front doors of the restaurant were flung open with enough force to break their hinges. Ignis came barreling out, her red flamenco skirt billowing.

"Terran female!" bellowed Ignis. "I challenge you!"

"Oh, hell," said Cindy.

Cragg intercepted Ignis. "This is Terra. Our traditions don't hold here."

"If she's dating a Saturnite warrior, she must prove herself worthy," said Ignis.

"She's worthy," said Cragg.

"Then have her face me in single combat," said Ignis.

Cindy measured her odds of surviving a one-on-one battle with Ignis as below calculating. Cindy had some self-defense courses under her belt, but they mostly involved kicking her attacker in the crotch, maybe gouging out their eyes with keys, and then running for safety.

"That's not the Terran way," said Cragg.

"Then you admit she's weak?" asked Ignis.

"Weak? She toils without glory in a world without the sense to appreciate her. She faces trials every day, an endless series of insults and ordeals that she has no true power over. Her enemy is stronger than her, overpowering, undefeatable, and still she continues to fight it. She can never win. She can only fight. And she fights on, even after knowing a hundred defeats. If she were a Saturnite, her quiet courage and endless endurance would be enough to defeat the Great Hordes of the Black Stone Dessert by will and stubborn resolve alone, and should it not be, I would be honored to stand with her in that magnificent battle and be crushed to rubble by her side. Where you see weakness, Ignis, I see only strength worthy of the greatest soldiers I have ever known. Do you think she fears your physical might?"

"Actually, I kind of do," mumbled Cindy.

Cragg laughed. "You can smash her frail fleshy body easily enough, but you will never destroy the warrior's magma that boils in her core."

He stepped aside.

Cindy and Ignis stood before one another.

"I hate to say anything after that inspiring speech," said Cindy, "but I'm rather fond of my frail fleshy body."

Ignis grunted.

"It's not even really a date," added Cindy.

Ignis bent down. Cindy could see herself reflected in the Saturnite's polished obsidian face. "Crushing you is beneath me." With a huff, she turned and marched back into the restaurant.

Cindy allowed herself to breathe again. Cragg was already lumbering toward his truck. When he heard the clopping of her heels, he stopped to allow her to catch up.

"I thought for sure she was going to kill me," she said.

"She was testing me, not you. She knows there's no glory in squashing an unarmed Terran."

"Oh. That's a relief. You could've told me that."

She grabbed his sleeve, and he stopped.

"All that stuff you told her, did you mean it?"

"Yes."

She motioned for him to lean down and planted a kiss on his cheek. Or the right side of his square head, which was the closet equivalent. It was like kissing smooth pavement, but not quite as gravelly.

"Thanks. That was a really sweet thing to say. So are you doing anything Saturday?"

Smiling, Cragg said, "I am now."

She took his arm as they strolled toward his truck.

IMOGEN'S EPIC DAY

Helen and Troy's Epic Road Quest

The original novel explores the idea of a heroic journey, updated for the modern world and well aware of itself. This story, featuring Troy's sister, Imogen, is the hero's journey squished into a concentrated narrative. It's The Lord of the Rings *without all the walking and* The Epic of Gilgamesh *without all the angst. In a thousand years, will it still be told around campfires by the robots that inevitably destroy and replace us? Who can say?*

(I can. Yes. Yes, it will be.)

The delivery guy stood ramrod straight with the exaggerated smile of a mannequin. His teeth were so white, Imogen was fairly certain they were all plastic, and his skin was so smooth, it could've been made of wax. There wasn't a wrinkle on his green uniform, and if he didn't move, it would've been easy to mistake him for a statue. He might've been good-looking if the universe had bothered to upgrade his resolution, but right now, the only thing completely human about him was his smoldering gray eyes. Nestled among his other features, it only made him more unsettling.

"Miss Imogen Kawakami?" he asked. His voice was deep and smooth, entrancing.

She nodded. "That's me."

"I have a delivery for you."

He held out a small package wrapped in brown paper to her, but she didn't take it.

"I didn't order anything," she said.

"Is your name Imogen Kawakami?" he asked, never dropping his smile.

"Yes, but—"

"Then this is for you, Ms. Kawakami." He thrust the package at her again, more insistently this time.

"But I didn't order—"

Imogen's roommate, Virginia, called from the living room. "Oh, just sign for it already! How many Imogen Kawakamis can there be in this world?"

Imogen couldn't dispute the logic, so she signed.

The delivery guy tipped his hat to her. "Good luck, Ms. Kawakami."

Distracted by the package wrapped in brown paper, she didn't notice it was a weird thing to say. "Thanks."

Whistling, he strolled away, swinging his arms and swaying his shoulders in a manner more befitting a cartoon character than a human being. He climbed into his green truck, waving at her, friendly if a bit mechanically, before driving off. Imogen closed her door and joined Virginia in the living room.

Imogen sat on their old sofa, and Virginia looked over her book and lowered her glasses to the end of her nose.

"What is it?"

Imogen shrugged. "Don't know." She turned it over. "This doesn't even have an address on it. Doesn't even have my name. The guy must've made a mistake."

"Maybe it's an asp," said Virginia. "Have any enemies I should know about?"

Imogen smiled and batted her eyelashes. "Who, me? I'm delightful. Everybody loves me."

"Must be nice."

Virginia was a cute nerd in exactly the way Hollywood liked to portray them. She was short but adorable with blonde hair tied up in a scrunchy-bound ponytail and freckled cheeks. She even dressed in slacks and button up shirts with suspenders to complete the look. But this wasn't a movie, and everybody knew she was beautiful. Technically, Imogen was the "hot" one of the pair, but Virginia was never hurting for attention.

Imogen put the box to her ear and shook it.

"You should open it," said Virginia.

"Okay, but don't blame me if there's a poisonous viper running around."

She tore open the paper and opened the small box. It took some effort to tear through all the tape, and she would've saved herself a lot of trouble if she'd just grabbed a pair of scissors from the kitchen. But by the time she'd thought of that, she'd already invested a bunch of time in tearing away the tape with her bare hands, and it seemed a shame to admit defeat at that point. What could've been accomplished in seconds with a sharpened edge took her four minutes of frustrated muttering, but it also felt all the most satisfying when she got it opened.

It was a cheap blue vase. She thought it was empty at first, but some dirt came spilling out of it when she picked it up, and when she shook it, the contents shifted.

"Weird. There's no note or anything."

"Weird," agreed Virginia.

Someone rang the doorbell. Imogen set the vase on the coffee table and answered the door. A woman in a buttoned down black suit stood on the porch.

"Can I help you?" asked Imogen.

"No, but I can help you." The woman flashed a strange badge, but it was one Imogen had a passing familiarity with. "Agent Campbell, NQB."

"You're with the Questing Bureau."

Campbell nodded so subtly, Imogen didn't even notice. "I believe I just said that Ms. Kawakami."

Imogen said, "Oh gods above, don't tell me my brother is on another quest."

"No, Ms. Kawakami. You are."

"Me?" Imogen laughed. "You have got to be kidding me."

Agent Campbell's face remained an inscrutable blank. "May I come in?"

Imogen invited Campbell in, guided her into the living room, and introduced her to Virginia. They offered Campbell a seat, but she refused. She stood with her hands behind her back.

"I don't want to tell you your job, Agent Campbell," said Imogen, "but I don't think I'm on a quest."

"The package you signed for," said Campbell. "Did you open it?"

Imogen pointed to the vase. "Yes, but that was all it had in it."

Campbell removed a notebook from inside her jacket and scribbled something in it. "And tell me, did you at first refuse the delivery?"

Imogen nodded.

Campbell made a noncommittal noise and wrote something else down.

"What are you writing there?" asked Virginia.

"Oh, nothing important." Campbell tucked the notebook away.

"I don't want to sound skeptical," said Virginia, "but didn't Imogen's brother already end up drafted on a quest? What are the odds that she'd also end up with one?"

"Better than you might expect. Those associated with greatness often end up picking up some of that greatness themselves."

Imogen leaned back and smiled. "Hear that? I'm great. Officially."

"Bully for you," said Virginia. "But I bet transitive greatness isn't as great as original greatness."

"Oh, you're just jealous. Although if I'm transitively great, then you're probably transitively transitively great right now."

"So you're suggesting I'm really really good."

"Better than nothing," said Imogen. "Where am I off to, Agent Campbell? What exotic location shall I discover? What strange and mysterious artifacts shall I seek?"

Campbell said, "We believe you won't have to go anywhere on this one. All indications are that this shall be a micro event."

"Micro." Virginia chuckled. "Way to go, Great One."

Imogen's smile faded. "What's that mean?"

"It's a bit technical," said Campbell, "but not all quests are epic journeys. Some are more localized."

Something thumped overhead.

Campbell reached into the pocket on the other side of her jacket and offered Imogen a small flashlight. "You'll need this."

Then she checked something else off in her notebook.

***

Virginia had been living in the old house for about a year longer than Imogen, who had answered her ad for a roommate when the previous one had moved onto greener pastures. But neither had set foot in the attic. It was a dark and spooky place, and while neither woman was especially superstitious, they'd struck an unspoken agreement to leave the forbidden space to the mysteries that dwelt within that shadowy realm.

Now they stood beneath the trapdoor, and listened as something moved around up there.

"What is it?" asked Virginia.

Campbell offered no reply.

"Is it a monster? Is it a hydra? A lion with skin that cannot be pierced?" Virginia whispered. "Some manner of attic-dwelling medusa?"

"Gorgon," said Campbell. "Medusa was the name of a specific

monster. Gorgons are the broader category. Like Pegasus was a specific winged horse, not a name for all winged horses."

The unnamed thing in the attic caused a floorboard to creek.

"Oh, we are not going up there," said Virginia. "It was bad enough when I thought there were only rats up there."

Imogen pulled down the extendable ladder.

"You can't be serious." Virginia grabbed Imogen's arm. "I'm not letting you go up there."

"Somebody has to," said Imogen.

"So we'll call an exterminator. Let the pest control guy fight the minotaur."

"Hey, my brother is dating a minotaur. She's cool."

"Sorry, but you know what I mean."

"Yeah, it's like that story where Thor had Bob's Big Bug Busters come and fight the Midgard Serpent for him. I love that one."

Imogen climbed the ladder and pushed on the trapdoor. It opened easily without even a squeak of its rusty old hinges. While Virginia mumbled from below, Imogen stuck her head into the attic and swept it with her flashlight. It was still pretty damned spooky, and even a little spookier considering she now was on a quest. Before she could talk herself out of it, she entered the dark space.

"Are you still there?" shouted Virginia. "Or did it eat you yet?"

"No, I'm fine." A quick scan of the space confirmed to her that the mysterious thing lurking in the attic couldn't have been that big. There weren't that many places for it to hide. Only a few steamer trunks, old boxes, and, of course, a dusty old wedding dress on a dummy because it wouldn't have been a creepy old attic without one of those.

The trapdoor slammed shut, and Imogen, despite herself, squealed in muted terror. The dread thing in here with her scampered from one darkened corner to another. Imogen went over to the door, held her miniature flashlight in her teeth, and yanked on the trapdoor. It budged a little.

Her foe scampered behind her, and she turned, trying to get a good look at it. It was too fast, but it also wasn't very big, so she decided she wasn't afraid of it. If it was truly dangerous, it'd stop screwing around and just attack her.

Virginia pounded on the door from below while Imogen tugged at it. The brass ring snapped off, so she resorted to digging her fingers in the crack, breaking some nails in the process. She'd just painted her nails, so that pissed her off.

The creature dashed toward her in the dark, and she whirled, catching it in the light.

It was only a rat. Not an especially terrifying one either. There was something tangled up in its tail. It glinted in the light. The rat stared at her with its beady reflective eyes.

"Yeah, okay. So I bet that's for me, right?"

The rat wiggled its ears and twitched its nose in a way that was almost cute.

"My brother gets to fight a god," she mused, "and I'm stuck with you."

Imogen had never been squeamish. As a kid, she'd picked up bugs and lizards with fearless abandon, and that skill served her well. She crept forward, only pouncing when she was close enough to have a shot.

She still missed by a good four feet, but as she lay there, embarrassed by her rusty tomboy talents, the glinting piece of metal must've come loose in the rat's flight. She grabbed it, tucked it in her pocket, and went back to the trapdoor. The third time was the charm, and it popped open.

Once out of the attic, she appraised her find, a small red vial on a chain.

"That's it?" asked Virginia. "You were almost killed by a monster for that?"

"It wasn't a monster," said Imogen. "It was only a rat."

"But we both heard it. It had to be bigger than that."

"Often our fears are worse than reality," said Agent Campbell helpfully.

"I really can never tell if she's serious," said Virginia.

"I think she's always serious," said Imogen.

***

The vial wouldn't unscrew.

"Lefty loosey," Virginia reminded Imogen.

"I'm aware." Imogen tried both directions, but neither worked. It seemed like a no brainer that whatever was in the vial needed to be poured into the vase.

"Are we doing something wrong?" Virginia asked Agent Campbell.

Campbell checked her notebook. "So far, so good."

Virginia tried to take a peek, but Campbell snapped it shut. "You don't want to see this. It'll only ruin the surprises."

"Easy for you to say," said Virginia. "This must be all old hat for you."

"Old hat?" repeated Imogen.

"It's an expression. And who says I want to be surprised?"

Imogen shrugged. "Oh, just go with it, Virginia."

Someone knocked on the front door, and they answered it. It was Rick, the guy who lived down the block. Tall, golden-haired, chiseled jawline Rick, as Virginia and Imogen had taken to calling him. It wasn't the best nickname, but it summarized everything they knew about him so far. That, and he also worked on cars on Sunday mornings. Imogen knew that because she timed her morning jog to coincide with the event, even though she hated getting up early, especially on Sunday. But he was just that good-looking.

She didn't have anything against asking most guys out herself, but a guy like Rick was so damned handsome, she felt like making the first move would've just been too easy for him. An ordinary guy, she could understand why they might be too intimidated to ask her out. But if Rick didn't ask her out, it meant he wasn't interested. She assumed he already had a girlfriend or was gay or maybe she just wasn't his type.

"Hi," he said. "Imogen and Virginia, right?"

Virginia practically squealed.

"Rick, right?" said Imogen, perhaps sounding a little too uncertain.

He nodded. "Yeah, so some friends of mine are coming over to have, like, a little get together, and we thought maybe we should invite over some of the neighbors. Get a chance to know them a little better."

"Some of the neighbors, huh?" asked Imogen.

He leaned against the doorframe with a coy smile. "Well, just the ones we were interested in getting to know better."

Virginia squealed again, without much effort to conceal it. "We've got some beers in the fridge we can bring over."

He looked at her and nodded. "That'd be awesome, Virginia."

Imogen recognized that look. Rick was interested in someone in this house, but it wasn't her.

Rick studied Agent Campbell. "You can bring your, uh, mom, too, I guess. If you want." It was plain he didn't mean that, but it was sweet of him to pretend.

"We'll be there," said Virginia.

Rick strolled away, and Imogen and Virginia watched his perfect ass sway on the verge of a swagger, but not so obvious as to be obnoxious about it. Campbell might have watched it too. Her dark glasses made it impossible to tell, but she did wear an ever-so-slight smile.

Virginia ran to her room and rummaged through her closet. Imogen sat on the door and watched her.

"What are you doing?" asked Virginia. "You should be getting ready."

"Can't go." Imogen held up the vial. "Kind of in the middle of something here."

"But this is Rick!" Virginia grabbed Imogen by the shoulders and shook her. "Rick!"

"Oh, I'm fully aware of who this is, but it doesn't really matter. He wasn't inviting me over anyway."

"What are you talking about? Of course he was inviting you. I mean . . . you're you. Every guy has a thing for you."

Imogen chuckled. It wasn't far off, and she had to admit, she was surprised when she wasn't a guy's first target. But she also was trying not to let that go to her head because there were a lot of people in this world, and some were bound to prefer the cute nerd over the tall, athletic type.

It wasn't like Rick was all that good looking. Not when she saw him up close. His shoulders were too wide, and his eyes were way too blue. It was distracting.

"If you think I'm going to stay here and screw around with you just because of some cosmic checklist," said Virginia, "you're out of your mind."

"No, I think you should go."

"I can't just leave you here alone."

"I won't be alone. I've got Campbell here. And the worst that's happened so far was that I had to scare a rat."

Virginia said, "But I can't. I just can't." She started picking through her closet. "It wouldn't be right. Do you think I should wear my red sneakers or blue?"

Imogen helped Virginia select an outfit and sent her on her way.

Campbell looked at her notebook, but she tapped her pen against her pad.

"Not worth a check?" asked Imogen.

"No, I think it qualifies," said Campbell. "Might have possibly skipped a step or two, but that's nothing to be concerned about."

Imogen sat on the sofa. If she listened closely, she could hear the sounds of music coming from down the block.

"Are you sure things are going like they should?" she asked Campbell. "We've been sitting here for two hours now without so much as an angry roach to show for it."

Campbell shrugged. "These things operate on their own time."

Imogen sighed. "I'm going to grab something to drink while we wait. Can I get you anything, Agent?"

"No, thanks."

"Suit yourself." Imogen went to the kitchen and opened the refrigerator. "Tell me something, Agent," she called into the living room while sorting through beverages. "Do you ever sit? You must sit sometime, right? How else do you drive?"

She grabbed a soda and returned to the living room. Campbell was gone. In her place, a tall and slender woman with chalk white skin, long red hair, wearing a charcoal pantsuit, stood. She held the vase in her hands.

"Oh, hello," said Imogen. It was a curious thing to say, but she said it mostly out of reflex.

The pale woman's skin was smooth as glass and even a little bit shiny. She turned her bright blue eyes on Imogen.

"The water, where is it?"

"You didn't happen to see another person here?" asked Imogen under the intruder's uncomfortable gaze. "Quiet, doesn't sit, not exactly a smiler."

"Didn't see her. Perhaps I was a bit rude. I am known as Safiria the Ancient, Exiled Emissary of Gods, Seeker of Power, The Merciless Lady, The Undying One, She Who Waits." She paused, handed Imogen a business card. "And The Prophet of Ages."

Imogen glanced at the card. "Wow. You managed to get all that on here."

"They work wonders at Kinko's," said Safiria. "Now give me the Waters of Life or else I shall be forced to make your life most miserable."

"If you're talking about this vial thing, I can't open it."

"I can."

Imogen reached into her pocket, felt the vial with her fingers. "Why is this so important?"

"That is none of your concern. Now give it to me before I lose my patience."

"No."

Safiria scowled. The glass flesh on her face cracked around the corners of her mouth. "How dare you defy me, foolish mortal child."

Imogen held up the vial. "I've read enough legends. I'm willing to bet if you could take this from me, you already would've."

Safiria groaned. "Oh, how I despise this age. This sort of thing was so much easier when you didn't all know the rules. You have no idea what forces you meddle with, child. Within this vase is the Glory Bloom, a sacred flower that was touched by the first drops of sunlight to bring warmth to this world. Older than even the gods above, it has within it unfathomable powers. And it will be mine."

Imogen tucked the vial back in her pocket. "Is this the part where you tempt me? Offer to make me an immortal goddess, free beer for life, maybe a new car?"

"Oh, I think we'll skip that part."

Safiria the Ancient snapped her fingers, and the front door exploded as a serpentine creature with fur, feathers, and scales in random patches slithered inside. It hissed at Imogen with its two serpent heads. Venom dripped from its fangs as it coiled its long, long body beside Safiria. The body was so long, it was still coming through the door.

"If you can't hurt me, why should I be afraid of your snake?" Imogen sounded more confident than she felt.

"Oh, it's not you I'm threatening."

The horrible two-headed snake monster finally pulled its tail end through the door. Virginia and Rick were clutched helplessly in its coils.

"Give me the Waters of Life now," said Safiria. "Or watch your friends die. The amphisbaena's bite is fatal and irreversible."

Each snake head hovered over the monster's prey.

"Don't do it," said Virginia. "I've read enough of these stories to know that giving the evil lady what she wants—"

The amphisbaena sank its long fangs into her shoulder. Virginia shrieked and fell limp. Her flesh turned a shade of green.

"Education is a worthy pursuit," said Safiria, "but it's no substitute for practical experience. Now, give me the waters that I might bring the Glory Bloom to flower. And in return, I shall restore your friend to life."

"But you said it's irreversible."

"All things are possible for the bearer of the Bloom."

Imogen clutched the vial tighter. "How do I know I can trust you?"

"What other choice to you have? Or shall I make an example of every poor fortunate mortal on this block? In this city? Starting with this handsome specimen here?"

The amphisbaena clucked eagerly as it pressed a fang against Rick's throat, just shy of piercing the skin. He wriggled in its coils.

"Aw, shit, Rick. I'm really sorry about this," said Imogen.

She twisted the vial in her hands. The cap loosened easily.

"The waters," said Safiria. "Now!"

"You want them. They're all yours."

Imogen twisted off the cap and splashed the droplets of water in the pale sorceress's face. Safiria howled as her pale flesh bubbled and cracked. Her monster serpent squawked and convulsed as its master fell to her knees and shattered, piece by piece.

"Cursed, child," she hissed. "How could you know? How? How?"

"I've seen The Wizard of Oz," replied Imogen. "Witches and water don't mix."

Only a torso, one crumbling arm, and half a broken face, Safiria sneered. "That isn't a weakness of witches. And I'm no witch."

"It isn't?" Imogen shrugged. "Oh, well, it worked didn't it?"

Safiria the Ancient grumbled, "What a world! What a world!"

She crumbled into a tidy pile of porcelain chips. The amphisbaena uttered one feeble cluck before transforming into a cloud of yellow smoke and drifting away.

"You can't tell me she didn't do that on purpose," said Imogen to Rick, who stood there in silent shock.

Virginia groaned. Imogen knelt down and cradled her. "No, no. There has to be something left." She put the vial to Virginia's lips and shook it. "Come on. Just a couple of drops at the bottom. I know you're there."

Virginia ran her tongue along her moistened lips. The green faded from her cheeks, and the wounds on her shoulder closed. She opened her eyes and sat up.

"Was I just dead?"

"Yes, you were," said Agent Campbell, now sitting on their sofa.

***

The National Questing Bureau agents swept the remains of Safiria the Ancient into a large Tupperware container. Another pair of NQB personnel busily worked at restoring the front door.

"Awfully nice of you to do that," said Imogen.

"It's what we're here for," said Agent Campbell. "Questing is disruptive enough without having to manage those little details."

"Am I immortal now?" asked Virginia.

"Temporarily."

"Temporarily immortal? Isn't that an oxymoron?"

"You would think so."

"What about that?" Imogen pointed to the Glory Bloom, or rather the cheap vase that contained it.

"Keep it," said Campbell. "The Bloom can't grow without the Waters of Life, and those are gone. Not forever. But for at least another thousand years."

"Just out of curiosity, what would've happened if I'd given Safiria the waters?"

"Can't honestly say, but it's just good policy to keep such power out of the reach of . . . well, perhaps everyone. Even the gods above." Campbell shook their hands. "You handled yourself ably. I'd put you up for commendations if we gave those out."

She handed each of them a card with her name and number on it. "Don't hesitate to call if the need arises."

"But I thought the quest was over?" said Virginia.

"This quest is." Campbell smiled enigmatically. "But there are always others."

The NQB agents finished their collection and repairs and vanished without a fuss. The house was actually cleaner than it had been at the start of the day. Imogen and Virginia sat on the sofa.

"Well, that was something," said Virginia.

"Yeah. Something," agreed Imogen.

"Thanks for using the last of the water on me."

"No problem. So do you think Rick still wants us to drop by his party?"

"I think that's probably unlikely," said Virginia.

"Too bad. He was cute."

"Forget him. If one giant two-headed snake chicken monster is enough to freak him out, he's not as cool as I thought."

Imogen went into the kitchen.

"Too bad about the Glory Bloom!" called Virginia from the living room. "I wonder if it could do all the things that crazy witch said it could."

Imogen leaned against the fridge. She shook the vial containing the Waters of Life and dabbed it on the tip of her index finger. There was barely a drop left, but she suspected it would be more than enough to bring the Bloom to flower. She pondered all the power, literally, at her fingertip.

"We should go out!" said Virginia. "Coming back from the dead makes a girl restless."

Imogen wiped the last of the Waters of Life on her pants leg and tossed the now empty vial onto the counter.

"Okay, but you're buying the first round!"

***

Outside the kitchen window, Agent Campbell, with the barest hint of a smile, checked off the final item on her list. She closed it shut with a snap, and whistling a cheery tune, walked off into the cool evening.

AFTERWORD

So that's it. The end.

When first undertaking this project, I'll admit that I mostly did for my loyal readers. They'd been clamoring for sequels for years, and I could only ignore them so long.

But a funny thing happened. I found myself enjoying revisiting my characters and worlds more than I thought I would. I still have plenty of original ideas to explore, but returning to see my old friends and add more depth to their lives was far more rewarding than I-expected. Does it mean more sequels are in the works?

Honestly, I can't say.

What I can say is that what I started with mild reservations ended with great satisfaction. I hope you enjoyed these stories as much as I enjoyed writing them. And if you should happen to have enjoyed them more than that, that's just fine by me too.

Be excellent to each other.

LEE

ABOUT THE AUTHOR

A. Lee Martinez has been writing for a long time and has even managed to get paid for it some of that time. He is mostly known for his irreverent style and obsession with putting weird characters in ordinary situations. He is most certainly human and not a cyborg from the future preparing the way for the Great Dinobot Uprising. Any time traveling soldiers from the year 3010 are lying if they suggest otherwise. Time travelers are notoriously untrustworthy.

CONTACT INFORMATION

A. Lee Martinez does not get nearly enough fan mail, and, like all public figures, is notoriously hungry for any praise you want to send his way. It would certainly make his day if you decided to contact him to tell him how awesome and / or good-looking he is, so go ahead and do that. You'll be glad you did.

FOLLOW HIM ON TWITTER: @ALeeMartinez
FRIEND HIM ON FACEBOOK: A. Lee Martinez
VISIT HIS WEBSITE: Aleemartinez.com
E-MAIL HIM DIRECTLY AT: Hipstercthulhu@hotmail.com

CPSIA information can be obtained
at www.ICGtesting.com
Printed in the USA
BVHW041647200120
569971BV00027B/2778